Orphans

The Novel

By

Arianna Miller

Published by Distinction Publishing House
Dover, Denver, Colorado
United States of America
www.distinctionpublishinghouse.cm

ISBN: 978-1-7374023-7-4

This book is printed on acid-free paper.

Printed in the United States of America

Dedication

To my Mom, Dad
And of course
To Kristina,
Thank you!

You are my ENTIRE WORLD!

Acknowledgements

I would like to thank my parents, Diarra and Velma Miller;
My little brother Nicolas for not ALWAYS fighting with me
while I worked;

My extended family members;

My teachers - Mrs. Turnquest, Mrs. Adderley, Mrs. Minns, Mrs. Stubbs
and Mrs. Carey-Campbell;

My editors - Grammy (Miriam Miller) and Professor Krista Walkes-
Francis, who worked efficiently to make sure that my thoughts were clear
and flowed smoothly;

Distinction Publishing House for believing in my work
and for facilitating the publishing of my first book;

Additionally, I would like to acknowledge and thank my
deceased Papa, Eldric Miller, whose love of reading impacted me greatly;
and

I thank all of them for encouraging, critiquing and working with me to
help me write this book.

Table of Contents

CHAPTER 1

Who Are We?

Kristina and I are twins. Some people say that we "look like twins," but as far as I know, we don't look alike at all. My name is Ariel Collins, but everyone calls me Ari. It's the same with Kristina. We call her Kris most of the time. She always wears these black boots, and this makes her look a foot taller than me. It is humiliating. Honestly, I don't often wear shoes like that because I never seem to find the right ones. I would rather wear vintage shades or a reindeer headband that glows - not that it is nowhere near Christmas.

All summer Kris and I had worked at the Moody Moon Hotel, which only had one moon, but the workers were moody. There was a girl who looked like she had just turned fourteen and was stealing from other people in the hotel while she worked. We made a few friends, and a little more enemies, like that girl who wanted to smash a tennis ball into our heads.

It was the beginning of September, and it was the very first day of school. I truly dread the first day of school, and it is not because of the subjects and all, my stress about grades or if there is going to be a new teacher (which there will be). It is because of one thing - our age.

The thing about our age is that we both just turned thirteen, at the same time (well, maybe a few minutes apart) and we are orphans. We did not have parents to help us sign any forms, but we did have a guardian - well, more like an older friend.

At the Moody Moon Hotel, we met a guy about eighteen or nineteen years old, and we stayed with him for a while because he was our Godmother's son. Our Godfather, who was supposed to take care of us, was probably wandering around New York City.

Anyway, Axel was the name of the guy we lived with again. He had blonde hair, and he was a foot taller than us. He was almost like an older brother. He made sure that, as preteens, we got summer jobs as maids' helpers, but he acted strangely. He also missed his mom, who wasn't dead but had been wrongfully imprisoned. One night he sneaked out of the hotel because he heard that his mother was released from prison. He did that without any warning. At least he left his signature on a note permitting us to go to school before he left. I woke up just in time to see him dart out of the door. Kris and I were kicked out of the hotel the very moment he left.

The alarm clock rang just as I yawned and stretched. Kris, on the other side of the bed, groaned. I turned off the alarm clock, almost falling off the bed. It was another day in Aunt Maybelle's apartment.

We were seven years old when our parents had just mysteriously died. We lived with our Godparents for three months. Then Aunt Maybelle finally had to step up and take us in. She had more than enough room in her apartment, which had three bedrooms, two bathrooms a living room, and a kitchen. She put us up in our own "apartment" -- that was only a spacious sitting room, a bedroom and a lovely bathroom. The problem was, Aunt Maybelle worked full-time, so she hired a full-time nanny to supervise us and Kasie, her daughter. The nanny's name was Natalie. She had been there for about five to six years (as long as we had) and would probably be there to care for us for many more years to come.

Kris got up and rolled over. Our bed was a complete mess.

"Shouldn't we make our bed like sophisticated teenagers?" I asked, trying to make her get the hint. Aunt Maybelle went bonkers over untidiness and Natalie detested messes even more than our Aunt did.

"We have plenty of time to do it," she whined.

"Whatever," I replied, and got ready to take a bath. "Get Kasie ready for school. And remember to keep her in HER UNIFORM. This is our third warning from the principal!"

Kris shouted something I could not make out and I crawled into a nice, steaming tub of water. We had enough pocket money to last us until next summer when we would work at the Moody Moon Hotel again. The only difference next year will be that we'll have to sleep in the servants' quarters instead of an air-conditioned, fluffy-bedded hotel room. I heard the phone ring, but I knew Kris had it.

Fifteen minutes later, I stepped out of the steaming bathroom with a white bathrobe around my waist and a towel **"smothering"** my hair.

Aunt Maybelle always raves about how our ancestors were Africans, so that is why we're the shade of a chocolate milkshake (not the real dark type, but more like regular light brown chocolate milk). I like chocolate milk, so I am fine with our skin color.

Half an hour later, Kris and I stood at the door of our elevator, waiting for it to come to our floor. I envisioned kids with all kinds of gross germs, picking their noses and having snot all over their hands. I shivered just picturing it. Just before the elevator door opened, I grabbed a can of Lysol spray and tucked it into my bag. I wasn't going down with germs without a fight.

The halls of our school seemed unending. There were pillars with huge spacing between them. Every time I go there, I always think the same thing. Our school's hallways are as big as stadiums.

While I was busy making breakfast, Kristina had gotten Kasie all dressed (or so I thought) in her uniform.

We walked inside the school. As the familiar staircases and open spaces came into view, Kris and I saw something strange and gross. A puppy was crouched in a garbage can with a little banana peel on his right ear. I stepped forward, and so did Kris.

There was a girl with long chestnut brown hair that reached her shoulders. My hair is waaaay curlier; it's black and it reaches my **"behind."** Today, I had it in a couple of buns with pink and purple scrunchies, that matched my pink and purple shirt. I thought I looked cute. The girl probably didn't care. She leaned into the trash can and took the puppy out. My hand frantically searched in my schoolbag for my Lysol spray. "Aww," the girl said, stroking its infected-looking head. "Why would anyone put you in here?"

"To decrease their chances of getting rabies, perhaps?" I mumbled, approaching her slowly but surely. The girl looked at me sideways. Kris came toward her and asked: "What animal are you?" I thought she meant the dog, but she was addressing the girl. Poor Kris, the girl will think she's **"off her rockers"** I thought. Instead, the girl looked Kris directly in the eye and replied: "Wolf, I am a wolf. What are you?"

Kris smiled like this girl wasn't crazy and said: "Lion." I realized they were probably talking about something Kris had mentioned to me about spirit animals. I didn't know what mine was, but I didn't like the fact Kris said I was a 'rat' because I wanted the last Snickerdoodle cookie. What girl likes her sister telling kids that her personality is like a rodent?

I gazed wearily at the two. They seemed to be made for each other. I sighed and turned around and threw pebbles across the small stream that was near the school.

The hall was filled with normal people. Some people were chewing gum and bumping other people in greeting. I groaned. "What's your problem, girl?" Kris asked. I kicked a ball of paper that was on the floor and whined: "This school is so dead. Nothing happens." I gazed at the endless white walls.

"Mmm," Kris grunted.

I couldn't remember what our first class was. I just stared at Kris, who was still hanging out with the girl with the puppy who was with a boy with chestnut brown hair as well, eventually revealed to be her brother. "He says he's a lion." Kris smiled and fixed her shoe.

"Cool," she mumbled, I'm a lion too."

The girl with the puppy's name was Cindy and her brother's name was Drexel. Drexel looked down at his flaming red tennis shoes. "At first I thought I was a snake and was pretty disappointed when I wasn't." He shifted his gaze to me, as I was staring at them. "Then I realized that lions are pretty cool," Drexel said. "I mean, they're practically the kings of the jungle."

"It's so weird how they don't live in the jungle," Cindy muttered. "Girl," Kris began, "One time me and my sis, Ari, were in a jungle."

"Sweet," Drexel cried, "what happened?"

Kris looked down at her lap. "Not muuuuch," she admitted.

"But I can tell you I saw a lion hiding around in the vines."

"Did not!" Cindy shrieked.

"Did so!" Kris shot back.

Cindy pouted and crossed her arms. She was a year younger than us. Drexel shoved his elbow into Cindy's ribs. I do something similar with Kris if she does anything inappropriate or disgusting in public. Kris elbows me sometimes, but mostly she says "C'mon!" instead. Cindy looked out of the window. "What did it look like?" she asked. Kris thought for a moment. "It was yellow and orange, like a lion." Cindy looked at Kris with a sort of pinched, dirty expression. "Gosh, girl, what did you expect me to say? It was red with purple stripes?" Cindy nodded, and I wondered if Cindy was cracked.

Wandering in the hallway, Kris grabbed me by the hand and said: "C'mon, girl." I followed her into an empty classroom. She fell by losing her step on several tables and chairs stacked in a corner. Because there were so many, only half of her body was left sticking out.

"Oops," Kris said. "Umm…"

"Buddy," I said as I stared at her. "You're on your own." I ran down the hall and got ready for the next period.

The teacher gave us a piece of paper to write down some things about ourselves. As I was writing down my favorite color, in popped a teacher who beckoned Kris to follow her. Uh-oh. That wasn't a good sign. "ARI!" Kris screamed. I was about to circle the word "hobbies" because the teacher had misspelt it. I pushed back my chair and reluctantly followed Kris and the teacher out of the door.

CHAPTER 2

Adventure

I tapped my foot impatiently and waited for Ari to come. This was great. Only the first day of school and we were already in trouble. The teacher had gone to stop some children who looked like they were trying to break into somebody else's locker.

I knew that Ari wouldn't be happy that Kasie was in her favorite pastel long-sleeve shirt with a unicorn on it.

I shifted from one foot to the other. "Why didn't you tell me you weren't wearing your uniform?" I asked. Kasie examined her sneakers and bent down on the floor to tie them. She was only seven, and six years younger than Ari and me, but she was unbearable. I took a deep breath and said in a much louder voice: "Now Mr. Smith is going to suspend you and Ari and me. Do you want that?"

Kasie looked up. "Who's Mr. Smith?"

Kasie had never been in detention. When Ari and I were in the fifth grade we caught a huge spider. It escaped from my desk and crawled onto our teacher, Miss Simon's desk. Miss Simon was allergic to spider bites, unfortunately, so her arm swelled up and became purple. She had to go to the hospital. Ari and I were on the verge of expulsion when we told Mr. Smith it wasn't meant to be one of our many pranks and that we wanted to take it home for our pet. We were lectured repeatedly.

"Mr. Smith is your new principal who can suspend and expel you. And both of those facts have something to do with Auntie Maybelle whipping us, 'kay?"

"What happened to Mrs. Williams?" Kasie prodded.

"She's having the time of her life without kids. But this principal is filling in, so we want to make a good impression on him, 'Kay? Suck up. Suck. Up. The…"

Just then Ari skipped down the hallway and so did my heart. Even though we were in trouble, if we got suspended, it would only be for about one or two days. In the meantime, if Natalie lets us go anywhere besides our apartment, maybe Ari and I could check out some stuff Downtown.

"Hi, girl!" I rocked back and forth on my boots and then turned to our cousin. "This is our problem…"

"Oh, goodness. Kris, *why?*"

"Ummmm," I replied, "well, I forgot. That's all." I put my knuckles up to my face to hide my grin.

Ari wouldn't give up. "I specifically told you to put her in uniform, Kristina!"

"I said I didn't HEAR YOU!"

Ari narrowed her eyes at me. The teacher came back and directed the three of us to the principal's office. I stopped outside, took a breath, and walked in.

Mr. Smith was at his desk stapling some papers together.

"Ah!" He put away the paper and went to his computer. "The first case of the day."

Rats. I pulled up a chair and relaxed into it. Kasie sat in the other one and Ari stood. "So," Mr. Smith began, "what's going on here, what is the problem?"

While I was explaining the misfortune, Mr. Smith kept clicking on his computer. Finally, he leaned back and remarked:

"Ariel and Kristina…Collins, right?" We nodded. He continued reading: "Live with your aunt…Hmm, I see lately Kasie has been arriving at school, not in school uniform. It appears this has been going on for a while now…"

Silence. Then Mr. Smith gave Ari and me a choice. We could either have one hour of detention after school for three days or be suspended for a week.

Neither of the options seemed good. "Do you mean three days starting now or three days starting tomorrow?"

"Your choice," he replied.

Of course, I needed to take the lesser option. There was no way I would go and get myself suspended, and risk getting my report card jacked right up.

Before I could give my answer, Mr. Smith interrupted: "You know, since it's the first day of school, I'll let you two off the hook for now. But Kasie will have to go home early, and your guardian has to come after school so I can talk to them."

We thanked him and walked out of the door.

When I got back to class, there was a note on my desk. I flipped it open secretly and read the message:

U like seashells, right?
Sawyers Beach. They have legendary ones.
Come b4 they're all gone.
-Potato

I crumpled the paper and stuffed it into my desk. No way would I trust somebody who called themselves Potato. As the class progressed, however, I felt like I really couldn't focus. I kept on thinking of some prankster and tried to identify the handwriting. Nobody I knew came to mind.

When class was over, I was more than ready to throw the thing in the trash, but I hesitated. Collecting seashells was one of the things my parents did with Ari and me.

Fine, but if I did it, nobody should know that I was pranked or something like that.

Sawyers Beach.

Wasn't that near Downtown somewhere? I stuffed the note in my pocket for, you know, safekeeping.

CHAPTER 3

Becoming Butterflies

242kris: 3:21: Girl, listen up. When Nat goes to the office, go with her. When Mr. Smith and Nat are talking ask to use the girls' bathroom, ok?

Arielbeats: Why???	3:25 PM
242kris: I'll tell u later 😊	3:32 PM
Arielbeats: When do I go to the bathroom?	3:32 PM
242kris: 4 o clock. Don't be late.	3:35 PM
Arielbeats: ok	3:39 PM

After school, I paced around the bathroom impatiently. I also checked the text again. I was definitely in the right spot. *But where was Kris?!* She said to meet her near the bathrooms. I checked my watch. It was 4:19 PM. She was nineteen minutes late. Or was I too late?

Natalie and Mr. Smith were in the Principal's Office, talking about what horrible delinquents Kris and I were. Since Mr. Smith insisted that both of us should come to his office, Aunt Maybelle had no choice but to stay home to babysit Kasie. She's probably shut up in her office, typing vigorously.

"Hello."

I jumped back. It was Kristina. "Where were you?"

"I had to wait five minutes before Nat let me go." Kris brushed past me and into the bathroom. "Is anybody near here?" she whispered.

"The last teacher left five minutes ago," I told her. "The janitors are probably coming in half an hour. We're the only people in the school for now."

"Perfect," Kris smiled, opening the doors to the female bathroom. We stepped inside, and I carefully shut the door. "How come you took so long?" I demanded.

"I told you, Nat held me back," Kris replied, looking around to make sure nobody was around, "and I kept on hearing scuffling. Turns out it was a cat. By the way, we have to go Downtown after this." I nodded and looked at the surroundings.

I studied the sinks and stalls of our school's large bathroom. It was cleaner than most other schools or public bathrooms. "We're going to become butterflies!" Kris remarked happily, doing some sort of twirl.

I was confused but managed to reply: "That sounds a lot more interesting than going Downtown."

"Uh-huh." Kris walked up to a door in the girl's bathroom that stated: **"FEMALE STAFF ONLY."** Ooh-hoo hoo. I smiled as Kris began to open the door. It looked like our bathroom, except even fancier, with a hair dryer and a Wi-Fi box. We stepped inside and Kris snatched the hair dryer. Its plug dangled as she grabbed a white bottle with green writing.

Kris laid down the hair dryer and bottle. I skimmed over the bottle's name and stifled a laugh. It was meant to be some sort of baby powder, but last year on April Fool's Day, some of the kids met secretly to replace it with a light green powder. The victim was a second-grade teacher. She dusted some on herself, and her skin was green for an hour.

Kris plugged in the hair dryer with an extendable cord and handed it to me. "Now go in the showers," she instructed. Oblivious to what might happen, I headed in and turned it on.

The second it was on, I felt charged like lightning and stiffened up. I immediately grabbed the shower handle and turned it off. I literally expected my body to be on fire, but nothing happened. I walked out, hair dryer dripping and screamed when I saw my thick natural curls sticking straight up in the air like tree branches!!!

"Shhh!" Kris urged, putting a finger to her mouth. I stared at her in awe. "You nearly killed me!" I roared loudly.

"SHUSH!" Kris insisted, "and no. I would never kill you. It was on low; it couldn't have done much harm." I looked back toward my reflection; mouth ajar, ready to cry.

"Okay," Kris said as she walked over to the bottle, added tap water to it then shook it up. "Good. So now you just have to put this on your hair-"She took advantage of my moment of shock and poured the green slime all over my hair. I could feel it rippling down my neck and onto my clothes.

"Kris!" I screamed. The word echoed throughout the room, and it felt like everything was vibrating. I smacked the bottle out of her hands, and it fell onto the floor. Kris ducked down to rescue it and I instantly turned on the tap and placed my ruined hair under it. I could feel my hair slowly begin to fall on my scalp *WHERE IT BELONGED!* and could feel the disgusting green powder draining out.

"Noo!" Kris shrieked, "my masterpiece! Ari, STOP!" I flung my head out from under the waterspout. My scrunchies were in the sink, my buns were gone, and my curly hair was now hanging down my back and soaking my shirt. I gave a sigh of relief.

"You ruined everything!" Kris scolded through peals of laughter.

"You almost ruined *MY HAIR!*" I snapped, looking around for a towel. I found a white one on the floor and used it to dry off my thick, beloved black curls.

Kris shook her head. "Scaredy-cat," she taunted, grabbing the same hair dryer off the sink and turned it off. I focused on gently drying my hair with the towel without breaking it. "Why don't you want to become a butterfly?" The way Kris said that it sounded as if it were the most amazing thing in the entire world. I put the towel down.

"If I'm such a scaredy-cat, why don't you do it?" I questioned smartly. Kris flicked some buttons on the hair dryer. "Fine," she declared, "I will do it." The hair dryer made a **"whooshing"** sound as it was turned on. Kris stuck her head under the shower.

This was mad foolishness.

I heard a quick 'buzz' and then the shower turned off. Kris walked out, looking dazed but proud. Her hair looked just like mine did, and she was striking poses in the bathroom mirror.

"See?" Kris cried, "you *are* a scaredy cat."

Exasperated, I shook my head and sighed. "Whatever. I don't feel so well. I'm going home." The last sentence was the only truthful one.

"Okay." Kris sounded as if she didn't care. I left the Staff Bathroom and exited the Girl's Bathroom. I went over to the principal's office, knocked, and opened the door.

Mr. Smith was saying things about 'calendars and planning' when I interrupted: "Nat, I'm gonna head home, I don't feel very well."

"Okay," Natalie called back, "put the meat in the oven. I'll be back soon."

On the way home, I put my hair into a ponytail so Aunt Maybelle wouldn't notice how awful it looked.

When I arrived home, I was exhausted. Kasie was on the couch, knocked out. Aunt Maybelle busted out of her Office. "Thank you so much for coming," she said, putting on shoes and hurrying to leave. "I have a call in half an hour, and it would be so hard to follow up by phone." Then she was gone.

I went into the kitchen, put the meat on a tray and into the heated oven and went to the bedroom Kris and I shared. After putting a little oil on my frazzled hair, I fell asleep on the bed in a matter of seconds.

I woke up to the sound of knocking on the door. I got up, rolled off the bed, staggered into the living room and opened the door. My mouth swung open.

I barely recognized the person in front of me.

There was Kris, with green skin (thanks to the powder!!!) and hair. She was wearing all green clothes (I don't know where she found them) and she was even wearing a green band-aid on her knee to top it off.

I could not close my mouth. I was absolutely flabbergasted!

"Don't ask." Kris stepped out of the elevator a little. There was a tense silence. An awfully long, awkward silence. Then Kris commented: "We have to go Downtown now."

"I am *not* going out in public with you looking like that," I stated, still staring at her.

"But I'm a beautiful butterfly!" Kris protested, twirling again. I cringed." You are not a butterfly," I said, "you're an alien."

"Tee-hee," Kris giggled, then stopped. "Fine, I'll change." She went towards the bathroom to wipe off the powder, make her skin black and normal again and change into not-so-green-, not-so-weird clothes.

When she came out fifteen minutes later, she was looking more normal, and we headed out at 5:10 PM

CHAPTER 4

Seashells, Slendie & Halloween Candy

Ari and I were in jogging sweats; mine was orange and Ari's purple. We were going up the path, and I was checking our crumpled map to make sure we were heading toward Sawyers Beach. We were about to go up the hill when I felt a tug on my shoulder. I turned around to see a girl with brown braided buns in her hair. She was just a teensy, tiny bit younger than we were and had a stuffed unicorn tucked under her right arm.

Ari stopped walking.

"Can you help me please?" she asked bluntly.

"Not now," I answered hurriedly, "come on, Ari."

"Can you help me, *please?*" she repeated.

"No, sorry, I'm busy," I replied earnestly.

"Please? I need help with the new maze they put up yesterday." She was almost pleading now; her hands were clasped together as if she was saying a prayer.

"Sorry, I would help," I offered, "but right now I'm kinda busy." I shifted uncomfortably.

"She doesn't know how to do it, anyway," Ari added. My eyes opened wide. "I do too!" I protested.

"You get lost a lot in mazes," Ari claimed "We got lost once in a maze and would've died if we didn't find the exit. Which turned out to be THE ENTRANCE."

I rolled my eyes. The girl with the unicorn sighed, nodded, and turned away. We continued walking up the hill, making sure to look out for cars every now and then. Once we finished climbing the hill, we walked on the sidewalk that was half-covered with grass. After a while, Ari inquired: "Did I just see that girl round the corner?"

"No," I shook my head. It was probably true, but I didn't want to talk about her. I knew Unicorn Girl couldn't have been going back. It was something in the fakeness. Maybe she thought that we were actually going to the maze.

"I could bet ten gold bars that girl with the unicorn rounded the corner!" Ari shuddered. "This is creepy."

"It's your imagination," I told her. "Don't be scared." We rounded the corner hesitantly. Unicorn Girl wasn't there. I tried not to show my fear. "A…are we being stalked?" Ari asked shakily. I shook my head like I knew for sure.

Suddenly, Ari screamed.

I laughed. It was an old **Slenderman** thing sticking up in the ground. I jogged up to it and stooped down. There was a stick stuck in the ground between its feet which helped it stand up straight. It was dirty and old, and it was obvious it had been around since last year.

"What is that thing?" Ari took a step back.

"It's Slenderman." I smiled.

"Okay, I'm out," remarked Ari, turning to leave. Unicorn Girl suddenly reappeared and climbed onto the sketchy Slenderman, holding his neck, and swinging her legs as if he were a horse. "It's just a prop," she insisted, putting her unicorn on top of her head, between her two braided hair buns.

Ari took a step back. I began dancing in front of the Slenderman, waving my hands in his face and Unicorn Girl joined me, kicking poor

Slenderman's sides until they were broken and there were deep dents in his waist.

"Hii, Slendiieeee," I sang, "what are you doing? How's ya day going?" I stooped down. "Hey, Slendie. Ohhhh, Slendie."

"Yeah." Ari took a few more steps back. "Yeah, I'm gonna go." I grabbed her hand. "Noo, don't go!" I cried. "See? It's a prop it's not gonna hurt you."

Unicorn Girl put the unicorn in her hands, climbed down and gave Slenderman a big squeeze, then released him. Now there was a ring dent around his waist and two holes on his waist as well. Slendie was looking even more beat up than before.

"Come, girl." I tried to drag Ari a few steps closer.

"NO!" Ari screamed.

I dragged her closer still. Ari put her face in her hands. "Oh, I'm gonna get nightmares for weeks," she moaned into them. "Okay," I said, starting to get annoyed, "we've been here for way too long." I looked at the sky, which was getting darker by the second. Soon, it would be night. "We need to go." Ari looked at the Slenderman one last time and then caught up with me.

Unicorn Girl came with us and skipped in the front. Suddenly, her pocket buzzed. She held a phone up to her ear. When she was done, she turned to us and feebly muttered; "I have to go now. My mom said I have to come to dinner." She ran off behind us and high-fived Slenderman's hand so hard it came off as she kept running.

Poor Slendie, I thought. *Deep dent around his waist, two holes there as well, and now one hand missing. Unicorn Girl sure is destructive. I can see her wrecking a brand-new chair.*

We continued jogging and I began to tell Ari all about where we were going and that a kid had left me a note before class saying that seashells were at Sawyers Beach. I also added that the kid said the lady there gave out free candy.

"This sounds like a scam, Kris," Ari said, walking right through a pile of leaves.

"I know. I'm just going to see if there is candy."

Ari stopped. "It's late September, Kris," she reminded me.

"Yeah, and so?"

"Our part of the town celebrates Halloween early," Ari commented.

"*We* don't celebrate Halloween."

"I know." I kept on stepping and checked the sky again. The pink and purple clouds were telling me: *Hurry up, Kris.*

"The candy she's giving out can be *Halloween* candy!" Ari pointed out.

"Girl, it's not Halloween candy!" I insisted, "It's year-round candy. She gives it out during the New Year, Easter, Spring, Summer, Fall, and Christmas. Year ROUND!"

Ari shrugged. "Just saying."

I sighed. "It's almost seven o'clock!" I cried, "we have to hurry or else she's gonna close and go home!" I began running, with Ari right behind me. We went underneath a bridge for a few seconds and back into the dim sunlight once again. I kept on staring at the sky, daring it to go from orange to navy blue to black.

I froze. "Kasie!" I yelped aloud. Ari looked back quickly. "No, she's not here," I said, grabbing her shoulders, "I mean we left her at home! Kasie's home alone!!"

"Okay, now we really have to go back!" Ari began running and I grabbed her by the shoulders. "It's too late to go back now," I stated, "and when I say that I don't mean it's night. I mean that we've come too far just to go back."

Ari blinked, then reluctantly turned around. We kept on sprinting until I saw a light blue sign and read the bold black letters! "WE'RE HERE!" I screamed excitedly, and ran straight to the sand, feeling it fall between my fingers while Ari splashed her fingers in the sea.

"Mom and Dad said there were pretty shells here," I spoke excitedly, turning over the sand, but my voice slowly faded into disappointment. "But there are no shells," I added softly with a frown, then paused.

"That's alright!" Ari said enthusiastically, "that was years ago anyway; people probably already took 'em."

I nodded, got back up, and checked my watch. My eyes bulged open instantly. It was 5:09 PM when I began running around and didn't even see a shack. I helplessly stared at the sunset, feeling defeated.

Ari gasped. "I knew it!" she cried. "We're in a magic town! I knew it! Everything's too gorgeous to be real. The Unicorn is probably an angel. The whole shack thing seemed so…unreal to me. The lady who owns the shack reminds me of a fairy godmother, giving candy to children. That prop we saw was probably…just a prop… but have you seen the butterflies? They're so pretty! And…"

I saw a red jeep rolling by with music blaring out of it. I waved at the driver. She rolled down her window, and I ran up to her car standing a few feet away, making sure not to get kidnapped or anything like that.

"You want something?" the woman asked. Ari stopped talking and caught up with me. I nodded. "A kid in my class told me that some woman gave out candy at this beach," I recited politely, pointing to the sign.

"Can you give me some, please?" I pleaded, sounding a bit like Unicorn Girl.

"Unless it's Halloween candy," Ari added.

The lady stared at the sign, sighed, and shook her head. "Yeah, I'm her, but a bunch of kids came during school hours and took all of it. See ya, boogers!" She rolled up her window before I could stop her and drove away.

"She didn't talk like a fairy godmother," Ari muttered after a little bit.

"That's because she wasn't," I said.

"Who told you about her, anyway?" Ari asked, starting to go on the road to head home. I followed her and replied: "A kid who called himself Potato."

"You mean the biggest scammer in our grade?!" Ari cried. I stopped, then sighed. "Yeah, that was him. Did he change his handwriting or something?"

CHAPTER 5

Fire Escape

We finally arrived back home, after two hours of what seemed like never-ending jogging. Kasie, to our relief, was fast asleep on the couch. I grabbed a bag of cookies and Kris and I watched our favorite series on TV. Natalie, to her dismay, found out there was no more rice and made an emergency shopping trip to get some all flustered and frustrated. Aunt Maybelle called to say she would be home in half an hour, so the three of us were on our own for now.

It felt so good to finally be home that I didn't want to move. The air conditioner was a relief. Kasie was resting peacefully between us, snoring, and muttering something about ballet practice. Kris laughed and I smiled. A sudden thought sprung up in my mind and I grabbed a paper from my bag.

"Kris," I said, waving the paper anxiously in the air. "The school talent show is coming up!" Kris was distracted by something else, though, and it wasn't by ideas of what we should do for our act. "Hold on," she said, "I think somebody's at the door."

And indeed, somebody was. When Kristina opened it, a girl with long, dyed velvet hair had just stepped out of the elevator. She had a pink bag on her back that matched her dyed hair. Kris and I took a step back, a bit confused. Kasie rolled over and was abruptly awakened, so, when she saw the little girl, she screamed.

"Calm down!" Kristina scolded.

"Why is she here?" Kasie screamed. "Who is she?"

"Ari, who is she?"

"How am I supposed to know?"

Kris bent down to the child's height. "Where are your parents?" she asked softly.

"I just came here to give you cookies!" She had such an adorable voice. She reached into her backpack and held out a box of cookies, with, you guessed it, pink packaging.

Kris waved it away. "We don't want cookies, honey," she insisted, "we already have plenty." The little girl looked past us. "If your parents are home, I can give them a cookie."

"We don't want cookies!" Kristina repeated, trying to be patient. "Why are you giving out cookies at night?"

"Because that's when people have dinner, and after dinner you have dessert. If you have no dessert, you can get my cookie!" She smiled and held out the package again.

I shook my head. "Kris, just kick her out please."

Kristina turned to the girl and said firmly, "Go away." The girl shook her head and walked past us into the kitchen and clumsily placed the cookies on the counter. Kristina and I exchanged glances and Kris shrugged. "Do you want anything else?" the little girl inquired when she finished her long and hard struggle to put the cookies on the counter and arrange them.

Before we could say no, we heard footsteps. I stiffened and looked out of the peephole. Natalie was back. If she saw this strange kid in here, we would have been dead. No doubt about it. I quickly considered my options and roughly led the kid to a small white closet, shoved her inside and shut the door. Kris, who had been peeking out asked: "Where is she?"

"In the closet" I whispered. At that moment Natalie came in and complained about being tired like she usually did. She handed me the rice and told me to put it on the stove. "I'm going home," she muttered, opening, and closing the door. "See y'all tomorrow." She walked out. Kris suddenly blurted out: "I'm going to experiment with fire. For a…project."

My mind raced to the epic party I went to with a friend once. The house had gotten extremely hot, so we got some hoses and water balloons, and had an indoor water fight! We were dancing and forgetting that our feet were soaked in water. Eventually, the water decreased, and we splashed in the remains until a surprisingly loud voice activated the "Draining Mode" and sucked all the rest of the water from the floor. The draining mode was in case of flooding, so that went well, I guess.

Kristina, however, was as chirpy as a bird and turned on the stove like fire wasn't dangerous.

"How about a water experiment?" I started to turn off the stove when Kris stopped me. "It has to be a *fire* experiment," Kris said, turning the flames up higher, "you need to take risks!"

"I do take risks. I've seen the risks before." We didn't have any draining mode if our place was set on fire, so we shouldn't just take risks.

"Yeah, of course you have." With that, Kristina turned on all the burners again. She was so risky it was scary.

"Take risks, girl! Can't you just take risks?"

"I've seen what happens, though!"

Kris shook her head. She suddenly scrunched her nose and commented that she didn't like the silence. We headed over to the music box, and Kris changed the music.

I was about to change it again when something behind us burst into flames. Both Kris and I jumped back, and I gasped at what I saw. The couch and the kitchen were on fire. I dashed toward them while Kris went to let Kasie and the strange girl out of the closet. But she was nowhere to be found. After a frantic search, Kris found her crouching behind the broom closet. Kris hurried to get Kasie and shoved them both into the elevator.

"Wouldn't it be better to send them down the stairs?" I queried. The last time I checked, going down elevators when fires happened wasn't the safest evacuation method.

"The elevator's faster, isn't it?" Kris shouted back. I hopped and ducked under flames and managed to escape quite a few burns. The fire really wasn't touching me that much, but it was just spreading everywhere. I turned on the faucet full blast and looked for the fire extinguisher. Another burst of flames told me it was too late, and I screamed.

Kris came in while the water in the sink began to trickle down the counters. It made a tiny puddle on the floor that morphed into a thicker flow that did not help with extinguishing the flames. I realized this wasn't working. The fire was growing bigger and bigger, the atmosphere was getting hotter and hotter, and the tension was rising. While all of this was happening, a melancholy song played. The sweet, sad song blended in so well with what was happening.

I saw Kris hiding behind the couch. "What are you doing?" I screamed. Our apartment was on fire, and she was hiding. Tears slid down my cheeks. "It's too big! It's over." Kris's voice was low and small. Her face was tear-stained as well. The tears came faster and stronger. "You turned the stove on!" I screamed louder. The 'Lovely' song reached its highest and most dramatic part.

"Stop pointing fingers, girl!" Kris shot back.

I glanced behind me as the red and orange flames danced around. I pulled myself together and climbed behind the couch where Kris was. There we sat on the floor with both of our heads on our knees. The 'Lovely' song began to wind down but how I wished it would keep repeating itself on and on and on. There was a cracking then a gurgling sound. I didn't have to look up to see that the music player had been burnt.

Suddenly, Kris stood up. "I'm going." The house smelled like ashes. "Mom said- "the words blocked her throat. She went to the elevator, even though it was dangerous. I remembered what Mom's words were, but I couldn't think of them. Not now. I dashed out of the kitchen, went into the elevator, and saw it close in front of my eyes.

I didn't know where I was. It was nighttime, and there was a fountain glowing white and there were lights on the trees. There was a small spring that I could barely see and a small light pink bridge to get over the stream. I stumbled into some fancy park. I had no idea where Kris went, and I had no idea where my phone was to call her. Neither did I know where Kasie and the cookie girl were.

I went to the stream in the dark so nobody could see me. What I could see in my dark reflection was that my clothes were scorched. My colorful scrunchies were gone and so were my buns. I also saw another reflection. It was of a girl with dyed blue hair. She looked just like me. Her clothes were ragged and torn but her hair still looked intact. It looked a little wavy with blue tips. A boy with brown hair accompanied her. Her mouth literally just hung open.

"Are you from The Diamond Square?"

I shook my head. I felt too miserable. My throat was closed. What if I never got to see Kris again? My stomach clamped up. I decided secretly to myself that tomorrow I'd go back to our apartment and check it out. Not even a mountain could get in the way of my decision.

The girl with brown hair and dyed blue tips sat down next to me. "Are you sure? I don't tell on runaways."

Runaways? Diamond Square? What was wrong with these kids? Where were they from? "I don't know what The Diamond Square is," I confirmed.

The girl's eyebrows were raised, but she lowered them and held out a dirty hand. "My name's Selene, and that's (she pointed to the boy) Nathan."

I nodded. Nathan looked behind him. "Ok," he said. "Selene, I think we have to go." Selene nodded and smiled a farewell smile at me.

"Wait!" I called after them. They stopped running. Nathan tapped his foot. "What's The Diamond Square?" I asked them. Nathan looked at Selene. "It's almost like an orphanage," she answered. "But it's more like you're a servant. You serve visitors who always seem to have lots of money, with respect. It's awful. We only managed to escape it for a few hours. Nobody has ever escaped forever." She sighed.

"Me and my little Kris could escape," I informed them. It could've been the wind, but I thought I heard the boy mutter: "You must be crazy."

Selene shook her head repeatedly. "Never!" she cried. "There are guards, and more guards, and more guards."

"Me and Kris can escape anything," I persisted. "We've escaped school lots of times; it's just like The Diamond Square."

Nathan crossed his arms and shook his head. "Silly girl, you know school is nothing like where we're from." Selene nodded her head wildly.

"Oh, yes, it is," I protested. "There are security cameras, and those are much worse because guards blink, but security cameras never blink. When they do, though, it's to zoom in. There are also hall patrollers that guard the halls twenty-four seven. If you're caught you..." "You get thrown out of the window?" Selene asked.

"No," I answered, feeling like all the air inside of me was gone. "You get sent to the principal's office."

Nathan scoffed. "Let me guess, then the principal will say "naughty girls" and you'll stay with him for an hour?"

I crossed my arms just like Nathan. I was trying to get these kids to see how similar the school is to The Diamond Square.

"No," I said. "The Principal's Office is just like a dungeon. There's even a fire where you can roast marshmallows." Nathan and Selene shared a secret look.

"Marshmallows sound pretty good," Selene admitted.

"And" Nathan added, "compared to The Diamond Square, school sounds like a place with sunshine and rainbows. We're starving at The Diamond Square, sweeping floors and dusting bookshelves till we *drop*."

I turned away from him. "But they're so alike! I mean, they both have people in them!" There was no comment. "Well, me and my sister's apartment just set on fire."

Selene gasped in surprise. "How horrible!" Nathan didn't look sympathetic at all. For now, I needed to find Kris. I got up at the very same time Selene did. She brushed off her rags. "Just so you know," Selene said. "If something else that traumatic happens, you're welcome to stay in The Diamond Square."

I thanked her and walked off. From a distance I watched the two run off toward wherever The Diamond Square was. I silently wished that Kris was here, right next to me.

CHAPTER 6

Every Girl for Herself

I was freaking out and I was crouched right outside the apartment building, leaning against a wall to catch my breath. I suddenly began panicking. Where were Kasie and that girl? I rushed around in a circle. *My Aunt is going to kill me!* I thought. I covered my face with my hands and rocked back and forth. My eyes were stinging. I was responsible for Kasie and that girl! What would my aunt say if she knew…I needed to find Kasie! And that girl…I wanted to cry, but just before I could, I heard two familiar voices.

I looked up through watery eyes to see Cindy and Drexel walking my way. My heart almost literally flipped out of my chest. I was ever so happy to see Drexel and the obviously jealous-of-my-life Cindy. I was about to say something when I realized what I looked like—a scorched and burnt mess. While I was considering this Drexel called out: "Kristina!"

They hurried toward me, and suddenly I wished I could run away. When they arrived, Cindy looked me up and down and so did Drexel. "What happened?" Cindy asked.

"Long story short," I said, "I was babysitting my cousin, went to Downtown's maze, there was a fire, sent my cousin and some random girl down the elevator and now I'm here." They looked at me quizzically, so I added: "So basically me and Ari's apartment is on fire, and I've lost both my cousin, a random girl, and my sister."

"Sorry, Kristina," Drexel said. "Hey, are you still a lion? Oh, um, anyways, we would let both you and your sister stay at our house, but our parents are going away for a week."

"And our grandmother lives in the apartment," Cindy finished. "She's not good with strangers."

Drexel looked at the ground and kicked dust with his shoe. I felt my heart drop. I figured Cindy was lying, but I didn't say a word. The silence filled the air.

"We could ask her if you want," Drexel decided. "We can even show you where she hides the cookie jar. We'll tell her that you're a friend we met yesterday."

Cindy looked like she was about to scream "NO!." She looked at the ground. "But it's not like that's possible." Drexel gave Cindy a look, and I did as well, inside my head. That girl was everything but nice. So, what if she had a brother who was a lion? I squeezed my lips together.

Drexel motioned to me and then he walked a few yards away and I followed. I looked behind me before my third step and gave Cindy a teasing look.

Drexel looked at the ground as I approached him. "Sorry, Cindy isn't being nice. She just isn't the friend type, I guess."

I spoke up for Cindy without thinking. "She can be a pretty good friend, Drexel." I then began to change the subject. "Soo, about your lion." Drexel nodded and pushed back his sleeve. On his wrist were a chain and a golden lion with a crown attached. My jaw dropped-in disbelief.

Drexel shrugged. "My mom gave it to me. Have you heard about her?"

I shook my head repeatedly. I suddenly felt like I was being left hanging and that isn't really a good feeling. It's like when you try to give your teacher a high-five and they don't high-five you back.

Drexel shook his head. "When my mom was alive, she loved animals. She used to have these classes with all kinds of animal lovers just like me and Cindy. Every kid would tell my mom what their favorite animal was, but she never gave that animal bracelet to them. She looked at their personalities. Are you getting me?"

I nodded again. This story made me think of Pocahontas.

"Anyway," Drexel continued. "A girl may say her favorite animal is a parrot, but she's got to be really fast to figure out solutions and stop bad ideas from going too far and eating them up. Like a cheetah." That was cringy. Eating bad ideas up... "A boy might say his favorite animal is a snake. But he's ferocious and looks out for his pack and younger ones, like a lion." It took me a second to realize he was talking to himself. I waited for him to continue, but he didn't.

"Is that all?" I asked, a bit disappointed.

Drexel nodded. Cindy, from where she stood yards away began fake coughing loudly. I brought myself to reality. "I'm sorry if that story upsets you," Drexel said. 'I'm fine," I replied. "Anywaaay, adios amigo!" Drexel raised his eyebrows. "What about your house?"

"Apartment," I corrected him. "And me and Ari got this, boy! We have enough money to pay the bills and renovation costs." Drexel raised his brows again sky-high. "How much money do you guys even have?"

I hadn't expected that question. At least we had money. Rich people, rich people, rich people. "I don't know," I admitted. "We got around twenty dollars each, maybe a lil' more, I don't know." Drexel's eyebrows hit the ground. He shoved his hand through his hair. "Okaaaaaaaaay then. You'll be alright with twenty dollars?" I nodded. "You'll be able to live the rest of your life with twenty dollars? (twenty dollars, indeed. Hee hee!) I nodded. "You can't be serious." Drexel insisted. He was hesitant to leave. 'Don't worry about me," I assured him. "Me and Ari are going to be in our apartment soon enough. See you around! We're going to be A-OK!"

He couldn't accept that. "You guys probably won't be able to fix your apartment with twenty dollars! You'll probably have to stay with a relative that hates you and you will have an awful life because of that!"

I was about to ask Drexel to leave me alone when I spotted the familiar little figure of a girl. "Kasie!" I shouted. I ran over to her and gave her the biggest hug in the world. I nodded to the other girl. Drexel looked at me with concern in his eyes as I walked over to the telephone booth to call Kasie's mom. I ignored him and waited for the phone to ring. By now, the sun was already peeking up. I rubbed my eyes. Wow! A full 12 hours of sleep lost.

The phone sounded like it was frantically answered. I rubbed my eyes again. "Hello?" I yawned into the phone.

"KRISTINA!" my aunt shouted. "What happened? Is Kasie alright? You didn't answer any of my calls last night! Where is she?"

"Well, I…"

"She's hurt, isn't she? Ooh, I should've known! Your mama may not have believed in whipping, but this mama does!"

"Auntie, everything's fine. FINE. You know, there was just a little… fire."

"FIRE! You are only messing with your Auntie Maybelle, right? Right?"

I didn't answer. I looked down at Kasie. She was half-asleep and shivering but, what could I do about that? The phone was silent as well, so maybe Auntie Maybelle was processing what I was silently saying in my head.

"Where's Kasie." It was intended as a question, but it was a statement as well with those tones that only serious people can manage to pull out.

"She's with me, ma'am. Snug as a bug." At that moment Kasie popped her head out of my tattered clothing and screamed into the phone: "I'M BURNT AND STARVING AND DYING OF COLD!" Oh wow, what a traitor.

"Oh my! Kristina, where are you?"

Another red firetruck zoomed by with the siren getting louder by the second. I watched with fascination as firefighters marched into the building in a line to completely put out the smoldering fire. A news truck pulled up and a news reporter interrogated the owner of the apartment building. Why had he not asked the REAL victims some questions?

"Kristina, where are you?"

"Outside the apartment building, of course. Where else?"

Silence. Then ... "Miss Kristina, I thought I could trust you. But I should've just gotten a decent babysitter. Maybe that one with the blonde hair…"

"Olivia Zoonti?"

"Olivia Zoonti. Bless her sweet soul. I'll be home in 10 minutes. Don't move a step because I know you will."

Aunt Maybelle hung up hard, and I gently put the receiver back in its place. I got myself out of the phone booth and looked at our apartment. There was no fire, but the smoke was pouring out of the windows. Drexel was explaining to the fire department crew and the reporter who they should really question, and the owner of the apartment pouted and crossed his arms. That man really wanted to be on TV.

"This is Golden News on a golden day, interviewing one of the victims of a recent fire on Dayton Street. Tell me, how did this unfortunate event happen?"

I sucked in a deep breath. "I... it's all my fault." I began hysterically bawling. Wow, all that trash thinking about the apartment owner, and I can't say two sentences before losing it.

The reporter looked a little down. "Uh-huh…let's go back to the owner and manager of the apartment, Wesley May-Ham!" The crew turned their flashing cameras and large cushioned mics away. Kasie was resting peacefully on my knee. She was literally holding on for dear life. Slowly, I dried my tears.

Drexel was leaning against a white car, and I approached him. "Is that your car?" I asked, even though I already knew the answer and it was probably a stupid question. "Or-I mean, a relative's car?"

He shook his head. I nodded and wiped my nose.

I looked at the ground. "Your mom was cool, I guess. I'd want an animal bracelet." He nodded. "She was great. People said she was an animal magician.

"You said you're fine, sooo, I guess I'll see you at school today."

"Today?" It was tomorrow *already?* Everything that took place since the fire seemed days ago. Was it Tuesday already and not Saturday?

He smacked his forehead. "Oh, sorry. You guys probably still need to recover from the fire incident. I hope I see you Wednesday or next week then." He stopped leaning on the white car and began walking towards Cindy. Cindy put her arms around him, and Drexel hugged her back. They must be close. I went over to the phone booth and picked Kasie up from the cold concrete floor that was beginning to warm up.

A few minutes later I spotted Aunt Maybelle's car. She had cooled down a little. Before climbing in I remembered the random girl; she was also asleep, but right out in the entryway of the apartment. I picked her up and placed her in Aunt Maybelle's car as well.

"Who's she?" Aunt Maybelle asked.

"A girl who came into our apartment," I replied. "We have to find her mother; she's more silent than Kasie."

"When did they go to sleep last night?" The car pulled out of the driveway of our apartment and into the street just as I had buckled up.

"I have no idea." I was still shocked only a night had passed. "We arrived home at night, around eight or nine because I was showing Ari the Downtown stuff and decorations." I left out the part about skipping school. "Then the fire happened, and we had to leave our apartment. I didn't sleep either, I just rocked back and forth until the first hints of sunshine appeared." I suddenly leaned back in Aunt Maybelle's air-conditioned car and relaxed. Oh boy, that felt so good!

"Where's Ari?"

I answered without opening my eyes. "I don't know. It was every girl for herself." Great, now we had to find a strange girl's mother and my sister.

"The Crosswell Park is over there; should we look there?" I followed Aunt Maybelle's vague gesture over to a park. It looked like those fairy-tale forests. There was a pink bridge and a clear, babbling stream with those light-colored small butterflies that flew around it.

"Why would Ari go over there?" I asked faintly. I was so exhausted that I could barely move. I wondered how Ari felt now. Maybe she was sleeping.

"Because…It's a really beautiful park. Just look at that lake!" I nodded. It was. Aunt Maybelle turned to park near it. I unbuckled and got out after her and closed the door. Aunt Maybelle left the AC on.

There was a fountain in the middle of the park. I peeked inside and saw tons of dirty and clean, chipped, and smooth pennies resting peacefully at the bottom. I had a mind to put my hand in and take out a handful.

Lots of people were staring and a few kids were snickering. I remembered what I looked like and groaned. We shouldn't have come here. I glanced over at Aunt Maybelle, who was admiring the glistening lake and watching birds fly ahead. That lady only wanted to catch a few minutes of sightseeing! And thanks to my appearance now, I was the only *sight* people wanted to *see*. I wished there were a few sparkling curtains that were made of diamond-like beads to help me get away from the starers.

I stumbled upon a girl in burnt clothing just like mine. Our eyes got wider as we stared at each other before giving each other the biggest hug ever!

Aunt Maybelle had scolded us every second, saying that we were so irresponsible. The apartment owner said we would have to stay with someone else if we couldn't afford to pay for the damage. He was furious but at least he called the girl with the pink hair's mom for us.

We slowly opened the door, and the scorched beige thing revealed the most heartbreaking sight in the world. Our apartment was covered with ashes; it was disgusting, smoky and awful. Aunt Maybelle sighed and muttered: "Our only home, gone."

We stepped out, and my heart began pounding. Ari and I didn't say a word. I held on to a weak piece of wall and a spell of dizziness passed over me as I saw something I wished I never had.

My favorite boots, the ones I had worn since I was nine, even though they were much too big, were gone. They were a pile of ashes on the only stand I put them on. Tears flooded my eyes, and I bit my lip. Kasie didn't seem much concerned, but her mom murmured: "This is over forty-five thousand dollars' worth of damage. Forty-five thousand dollars… Relatives. I'm gonna start calling relatives. C'mon, Kasie." They went out of the door, leaving it cracked open. "You two," she instructed poking her head through the half-opened door, "see what can be salvaged while we're gone."

Ari gestured for me to come into the kitchen. There was a blanket that was now only a heap of black dust, exactly the way my boots now looked.

Ari sat down on top of the black dust heap, and I plopped down next to her. We sat in silence for a little bit, and as I surveyed all the officially ruined décor of our place, tears came back to my eyes. Ari was also wiping off her tear-stained face.

"I'm so sorry," I whispered.

"For what?" Ari tugged at the blackened sofa.

"For setting the apartment on fire. I'm a horrible sister."

Ari quickly shook her head. "No, you're not! You're the best sister in the world! You didn't make this fire happen!"

I was about to protest that I *did* when the phone rang loudly. In my "fear of the world," phase I was beginning to go through, I jumped up and hid behind Ari. I honestly felt like a baby. Ari skipped towards the telephone. It was in the back of a wooden closet, and it was still smoking as it rang.

"It might blow up," I warned her. "Don't answer it."

Ari shook her head. "What if it's something useful to us like an orphanage?" She suddenly gasped as she held the cordless phone in her hand and covered her mouth like she remembered something important. Then she put the phone to her ear. "Hello?"

The voice on the other end was so loud that both of us could hear it and Ari had to move the receiver from her ear. "Is this…let me see…Ari and Kris?" it buzzed. I nodded even though the person couldn't hear or see me. Ari almost nodded as well but said: "Y…yes." I nodded more firmly, feeling dizzy. A stranger was calling our house and it was after we had a fire!

The voice of the stranger was that of a male. "A-hah! I knew it! You two won't escape the law today!" Ari trembled and didn't say a word. *This is all your fault!* My mind was screaming. *This is all your fault!* The man continued: "You hid for too long, now you're setting fire to a public place!" Ari shook her head some more. "We didn't! We own this apartment…" Her voice was shaky and uncertain.

"No!" the man shouted. "No, we are not wrong! We're never wrong! Are you going to listen to me or not?!"

Ari looked at me with trembling lips. The stranger took our silence as a yes.

"Anyway," he continued. "If you don't have any family or friends willing to accommodate and house you, I will give you a recommendation. It's called the *streets.*"

Both Ari and I screamed "NO!" The streets are the worst. Cats would steal your food, and dogs would give you rabies. Your skeleton would be left in the open for people to walk or drive over. My eyes flooded again, and Ari's cheeks were wet.

"I'll be at your "place" (he said this sarcastically) in half an hour to give you a ride to your new home."

Ari and I were speechless until Ari mustered up the confidence to say, "NO! We worked hard at the Moody Moon Hotel, and we saved up enough money to get here! I'm not budging from my spot!"

"Yeah!" I chimed in, sounding like a mouse. "You're just a hateful man!"

"Yeah!" Ari said. "You had no childhood!" I began to cry.

The man sounded like he was chuckling. "Fun fact, not all fairy tales end happily ever after." He hung up.

We were two sisters.

We had a good life.

And now we were going to die.

CHAPTER 7

The Diamond Square

We couldn't pack anything. We didn't have the heart. Well, we did pack some things. Kris packed a photo of us working at the Moody Moon Hotel and some ashes in Ziplock bags (I have no idea why) and said it was precious to her. She also packed her license for the Moody Moon Hotel (because I reminded her to) so we could get off the streets and work there for a whole summer. I packed a photo of us, my license for Moody Moon, and a notebook. I've kept lots of notebooks in my life, but I thought that maybe I should write about my new life in the streets. That's all we packed. That's all we could pack without breaking down in tears.

We were in the back seat of the stranger's car, who honestly, looked exactly as I had pictured. He had sleek blackish-brownish hair that was obviously gelled down and smooth skin with no pimples or marks or anything. He never smiled until he saw the suffering on our faces.

I looked out the window and saw cars driving by, and people walking down the streets. I checked my watch, and it read 12:40 PM. I sighed for the millionth time.

Kris looked at her hands. "I'm so sorry, girl."

"Think about something else." I had run out of ways of soothing Kris. Deep down in a tiny, dark corner of my brain, I knew she was right, but nobody is perfect. Besides, I already knew that we weren't going to be in the streets for long. Eventually, Kris and I would stop crying like sad looney tunes and put our heads together to figure out how to get out of this fix.

The problem was I didn't know how.

The man suddenly stopped. "Here we are!" he announced. "The streets!" He glanced around at the rusty concrete and tile like it was something valuable.

"We've been seeing the streets for ages," I informed him. The man laughed. "You'll *love* your new humble abode. There's fresh street water and puddles you can lap up, that'll be delicious. And your local trash cans have all the types of food you can imagine, from chicken bones to bread to fries to sodas. OH! And there's a five-star reviewed concrete bed. It's amazing how the hard brick massages your bones. Ta ta!"

"Whatever," Kris said, hunched in the seat, glaring at the stranger. "Do what you want, you can't make our life any worse than it already is. Get lost!"

The stranger nodded. "Of course, of course! Out you go! Tata! Hasta La Vista! Now that you two are out of my schedule I can go on vacation!" He pushed us out, closed the door, and drove off laughing loudly and happily. We barely had enough time to grab what little stuff we had brought with us.

Kris sat on the ground and leaned against a huge rock. "Better get comfortable now, because we're going to be here for a very long time." I shook my head repeatedly, but I sat down. I refused to believe that.

I started thinking of The Diamond Square. What would it be like to live the life of a servant? I didn't know......I was looking forward to the Moody Moon more and more. If Kris and I managed to suck it up until summer, that would be three whole months of luxury and comfort. Sleeping in the workers' quarters sounded waaaay better than dusting bookshelves and sweeping floors until we dropped. Plus, if we worked at the Moody Moon, maybe we could get a new apartment.

But that was wishful thinking. Kris and I couldn't make it until summer. Maybe we'd be able to escape the Moody Moon when summer arrived and actually live a happy life. Maybe we could bring Selene and Nathan, I guess, if he was desperate. I would have to think about it some more.

I broke a piece of toast from my little bag of belongings and shared it with Kris. We nibbled on it for a little while.

"I don't feel very hungry," Kris said, putting down the toast.

"We'll die of starvation soon, anyway."

I shook my head. "No, we won't." Kris looked up from the piece of bread. "Girl, do you even know how the world works?" she asked. "We are going to die."

I shook my head. "Not exactly…."

"What do you mean not exactly…?"

"I have friends in hidden places."

The Diamond Square was hidden. Selene and Nathan were literally in a hidden place. It was hidden behind several tall buildings. Behind all those buildings, there was a dark staircase that led down to something.

As Kris and I climbed down the stairs, everything got darker and darker, and I was afraid something would reach out and grab me.

There was a dark train station. The train looked like it was about to fall apart. I walked over to it and slid my finger along the rusty thing. I examined my finger and saw that it was completely filthy. I wished that I still had my Lysol spray can with me.

I stepped back from the train. "How about we walk instead?"

Kris shook her head repeatedly. "I'm tired," she said, "and really confused about where we're going. I can't walk another step. I might pass out."

I sighed. From Nathan's description of The Diamond Square, we probably needed to store up all the energy we could and walking for miles didn't sound like an incredibly good way to do that. I knocked on the door of the train. A man who was underneath the train, his mud-covered boots sticking out on the other side, appeared immediately at the sound.

He didn't have incredibly good teeth (nothing that a little dental hygiene couldn't fix) and he was bald. He didn't look very amused, and I cringed.

"HEY!" he shouted. "Hey, you two! I ain't like to hear loud noises. Do you even *know* how loud that echoed in my ear-hearing thing-of-a-jigs?"

"No, we don't sir," I answered. "We have perfect hearing." Kris nodded and smiled.

The man wiped off his hands with his apron. "I'm thinking you two want a ride. Where are we going now?"

"To wherever this girl's idea leads us to," Kris said. She didn't even know what my plan was as yet! Not that she would even like it. I suddenly missed the Moody Moon more than ever.

"We want to go to The Diamond Square, sir."

"I shouldn't have even asked," the man sighed. "Any way that leads in the direction of The Diamond Square leads to your doom."

My heart thudded loudly in my chest.

Kris looked at me sideways. "Um, I think we're good now, sir." I ignored her and firmly told the man to take us to The Diamond Square. He nodded and we climbed onto the train.

The seats were torn. Some nasty odor was in the air. Some oily stuff dripped out of an out-of-place pipe.

Forty-five minutes later, we arrived at a huge gray building with gray bricks, gray concrete, gray everything. People in tattered and smelly clothing were either nailing up boards or carrying stuff to a huge trash can then going back to the building. Guards surrounded the outside. Nathan and Selene weren't kidding. It seemed like there were millions of people here.

Kris shuddered. "So, this is better than the streets?" she asked in disgust. "I'm telling you, that kid looked sick…"

"The garbage she was taking out looked gross, you can't really blame her."

Kris and I walked to the main door and opened it. Humans in tattered clothing, from kids to adults were scattered everywhere. There was a registration desk where a plump lady sat. She looked at us for a long time, like we were cockroaches, she was just daring to move.

"Well, darlings, hello, what brings you here?"

I looked at the floor. Kris thankfully jumped in and said: "We're getting jobs here, as--sla… I mean servants!"

I nudged Kris hard in the ribs. There goes any chance of getting special attention.

The lady checked a little book looking over her spectacles. "Mm… interesting." Her head suddenly sprang up. "Excuse me for one moment, young ladies." The middle-aged woman jumped up from her wooden chair and went into a dark hallway. The sound of a boy's screams echoed out. Then there was the sound of loud spanking. I'd never been spanked before but the screams from the boy were genuine. He was in real pain.

The plump lady screamed: "I TOLD YOU NOT TO EAT THAT! WHAT WILL MISTRESS EMILY EAT WHEN SHE ARRIVES TOMORROW?" The wailing rose to at least *two* more levels.

The plump lady's figure became more apparent as she went into the large opening room with the sun's light coming in through the windows.

She faked a smile as she walked back to her desk. She sat down all puffed out and taking big heaves. Then she opened a drawer and pulled out two pieces of paper. She pulled out two pens and instructed us to read the form and write our names on the pieces of paper. The form was all about promising to do our work, and if we did anything off, we were to be either kicked out on the streets (yaaaaay) or we were going to be spanked. The consequences got worse if we did worse things.

After 5 minutes of horrific reading, I signed my name. Kris was already finished and leaning on the desk. Something told me we didn't know what we were getting ourselves into.

The plump lady told us to call her Mrs. Sesmore. That would be hard to remember.

As Mrs. Sesmore began talking, I shifted my gaze over to the dark hallway and saw a boy finally emerging from it. He staggered and leaned against a wall for support. Then he ran into the arms of somebody else. They both looked familiar. I realized the boy who was beaten was Nathan, and the girl he was hugging for comfort was Selene.

I sucked in a deep breath.

Mrs. Sesmore gave us name tags and told Kris and me that we were officially working for The Diamond Square. I looked at Nathan and Selene, who were now walking away, and remembered the train driver's words.

"I shouldn't have even asked. Anywhere that leads there…leads to your doom."

So, as Kris and I grabbed our name tags and were walking to the lunchroom for a late lunch, I began regretting my decision to surrender both Kris and me to The Diamond Square. It finally hit me so hard that I almost stopped walking.

Welcome to your Doomsday.

The Lunchroom was another huge room with window lighting and a huge chandelier dangling dangerously above the middle tables. The tables were dirty picnic tables with gum stuck underneath them.

Today was, I had overheard, one of the lucky days because they normally don't have late lunch here. We only had a late lunch today because we were going to have a special guest. Wow, our first day of work at The Diamond Square and our first guest or guests as well!

"Just to get this straight, girl," Kris said. "We're here at this weird building to work and to have a place to stay until summer when we get to go back to the Moody Moon Hotel."

I nodded. "I also met two kids who are from here. I think we can rely on them until we can catch on." I had no idea what I was saying. Why would two random kids whom I met a few hours ago help us? At least Selene was nice. I didn't know if Nathan was or wasn't.

We got one slice of apple and half a bowl of disgusting-looking oatmeal then looked around the room to see where we should sit. There was a table near the corners of the room where Selene, Nathan and two other kids were sitting. Kris and I approached, and the children's eyes grew bigger. Nathan stopped gulping down his oatmeal and Selene stopped chewing on her one slice of apple.

"You're here," Selene said. "I can't believe it!"

"I can." Nathan stirred what was left of his oatmeal. His eyes were still red from sobbing. He avoided eye contact with everybody and ate silently.

Kris decided to introduce herself. "Hi," she said, looking directly at her apple slice. "Um, I'm Kristina, but you can call me Kris for short."

Selene nodded. "We know. We're Selene and Nathan." Then she turned towards me. "Speaking of names, what's yours?" Everybody waited for a response.

"Uh…Ari, I guess." *I guess? Don't I know my own name?*

The two other kids at the table finished at the very same time and left, rolling their eyes and giggling. One girl began to talk. "Carson's going to watch us clean." The other girl scoffed.

"Carson gets to do *everything*," she protested. "It's not fair."

I turned back to my table and asked who our guests were. Selene told me their names were Mistress Smith and Emily. Kris and I gave her a blank look.

"Two of our regular special guests," Selene explained. "We *were* going to give them a chocolate three-tier cake, but Nathan ate it." She giggled at the words while Nathan blushed and kept his head down. Kris laughed with Selene, and I kept my head down like Nathan. "Anyway," Selene continued, "they're coming tonight and we're not getting our slice of bread and tea for dinner so that's why we're having late lunch right now."

Nathan nodded.

A handsome boy with noticeably light blonde hair and blue eyes came into the room. He wasn't in tattered clothing, but the regular boy attire. He was wearing a red and white striped shirt with a hoodie and jeans. He stood on top of a table in the middle of the room and the kids who were sitting there scattered. Nathan rolled his eyes and Selene muttered something angrily.

Kris and I looked at him with interest. "As you all may know," he said. "Late lunch is officially over, and we are expecting guests tonight, so off to your dormitories. Shoo, now!"

Everybody grumbled as they finished spooning late lunch into their mouths or walking slowly out of the archway that was supposed to be a door.

As Selene talked about sharing dorms, I got chilling thoughts. *Welcome to your Doomyear. Welcome to your Doomsday. Welcome to your Doomsquare.*

Get it? Cause it's *The Diamond Square.*

CHAPTER 8

Emily

I was starting to like this place. I mean, nothing bad has happened yet; plus, Selene and Nathan were nice. The dorm wasn't as comfortable as I thought it would be, however. There were four beds (coincidence or not?) and there was a thin mattress with a thin blanket and thin pillows.

According to the big wall clock, it was 3:16 P.M. Time was flying. I adjusted my pillow behind my back even more. Nathan rolled over in his bed, and Selene hummed softly. Ari shifted loudly in her sheets.

A loud knock was heard on the door. I swung out of bed and my bare feet stepped onto the cold tile. I opened the door and saw Mrs. Sesmore (weird name) standing at our door with a clipboard in one hand. I smiled uneasily. We were going to have work already?! My uneasy smile became even more so.

"Good afternoon," Mrs. Sesmore said. Her face was chubby and red. "Aren't Selene and Nathan supposed to be here?"

"We're sharing this dorm with them," I explained. "Soo, what are we supposed to do?"

Mrs. Sesmore sighed. "You! There are four of you in there now, right? Well, the four of you are going to clean the silverware and mop the floors of the main dining hall, the one that has the big table with a red cloth covering it. The one with the chandelier, got it?"

I nodded and closed the door. I repeated the instructions Mrs. Sesmore had given me and we all left the dormitory and went to the closet to get all the dusters, brooms and mops to clean the main dining hall.

Fifteen minutes later we were doing our part to clean up the main dining hall. It was hard work. I mean, Ari and I aren't really slobs. We know what it is to clean, but a huge dining area that's almost as big as our apartment itself is a whole different story. I was on all fours, scrubbing the floors and almost completely stretched out. Selene and Nathan didn't seem to mind cleaning. They were probably used to it after years of being here.

"Know what?" I asked our unhappy group.

"What?" they chorused.

I turned to Selene. "Share something with us, girl."

Selene stopped sweeping the dirty floor. "Huh?"

"Come on, come on!" My behind collapsed onto the wet soapy ground, but I didn't care.

"You mean share something as in a secret?" Selene let go of the broom and wiped her hands on her apron. If I didn't know better, I would have said she was nervous. An uncontrollable grin split across my face.

As Selene opened her mouth, the same boy who had walked into the lunchroom strolled in. The way he walked reminded me of the hall patroller at school. I glanced outside a window (there were a lot of windows in this place) at the blue sky and wondered if Drexel and Cindy were expecting us to be at school tomorrow or even the day after, because I didn't think we were going anywhere for a long time. And this time, it was confirmed. My mind came back to the present and to the boy who was still in the doorway that wasn't really a doorway. It was just a curved entrance or opening resembling an arch-like shape, I guess.

He walked all around the room, patted Nathan on the head, and then attempted to hit a sponge right out of Ari's hand, but Selene whipped the boy with the mop before he could interfere. The boy winced and shot Selene a mean look. "You'll pay for that," he hissed.

Selene shrugged. "Have I ever?"

The boy skidded out of the archway to another room to torture other poor kids.

Nathan stopped cleaning and leaned against the wall. He had been a sourpuss ever since I met him. I scrubbed extra hard at a brown stain that wouldn't come off.

"How long have we been cleaning?" I asked.

"Half an hour maybe?" Selene assumed. "We'll probably be done any minute now because" … Just then a loud bell rang and a loud black speaker in the corner of the room announced: "MISTRESS SMITH AND EMILY HAVE ARRIVED. MEET AT THE MAIN HALL AND TRY TO LOOK PRESENTABLE. "

Then there was heavy breathing.

Selene and Nathan literally skidded out of the door and down the hall, so Ari and I dashed after them. We kept on running toward the main door. This was so stupid. If they were going to eat in the main dining hall, why didn't we just stay there? I inspected the floor as the tall doors opened.

A bougie girl around me and Ari's age and a woman stood at the entrance. The girl had huge blonde curls that hung peacefully down her back. Ari's was almost identical, but her hair had tighter and thicker curls and was black. The girl was wearing a sunhat and a flowing white dress. A flower stuck out of her hair. She held a white umbrella in her hand. White galore.

She was probably that Emily kid.

The boy who had barged in on our work made his way to the girl and said: "Carson Waite, very pleased to meet you." Then he kissed her on both cheeks, bowed and made his entrance. Ari and I made faces, and even though some people might think it was crazy, Ari hated romance just as much as I did.

Mistress Smith raised her brows and cleared her throat.

"Mr. Waite, if you don't mind, Emily is *much* too young for any sort of romance." Emily nodded her head in obvious agreement and wiped off her face with a little hanky taken from her little white purse swung around her neck.

A man with a shiny head, dressed formally stood right next to a mortified Carson, with his head hung low. "Where we come from, Mistress Smith," Mr. Waite declared in a booming voice, "that is a gesture of welcome, *not* I repeat *not* any type of romance." He slowly drew out the word romance, as if he didn't like the topic himself. Mistress Smith nodded reluctantly.

I couldn't possibly imagine any other place having to do that as a gesture of welcome. I also couldn't believe Carson and his *man* came from a foreign part of the world. I thought that they were just Americans.

"All students please go to the main dining hall," Mr. Waite declared. Who was this guy anyway? What if he wasn't as important as he seemed to be? "Um, excuse me." I'm highly aware my voice is shaking with fear. *Girl, Kris, keep it together.* I cleared my throat. "Um, well, I wondered who you were?" There was a loud, collective gasp. *Wow Kris, you just said something stupid.* I felt dizzy.

Mrs. Sesmore approached with a whip in her hand, but Mr. Waite put up his hand to stop her. Mrs. Sesmore stopped and stood still. Now I got it, Mrs. Sesmore bossed us around, but this Mr. Waite guy was clearly the boss of this building. "I" Mr. Waite began, "am Mr. Waite. I am the manager and leader of this estate." He nodded toward his son. "This is Carson Waite, and you are to treat him with respect as well."

I kept nodding at everything he said. Ari was staring at a wall and Selene and Nathan were still standing at attention. Mrs. Sesmore un-paused herself and gave Mistress Smith and Emily a seat at the table. Mr. Waite and Carson sat at the other end. Mrs. Sesmore gave Ari two trays and asked her to give them to Mr. Waite.

"You mean to that bald guy over there?" Ari pointed. There was yet another louder collective gasp. Mrs. Sesmore turned red. I looked down to hide my smile. Selene shook her head and Nathan slapped his forehead. Mr. Waite put his head down on the table and sighed loudly. So many things were happening at once! I waited for somebody to say something.

Mrs. Sesmore snatched the trays from Ari's hands and placed them gracefully in front of Mr. Waite and Carson. The trays included a whole turkey, mashed potatoes, and loose corn. She then hurried to the kitchen and brought out another two trays with identical food and gave them to Mistress Smith and Emily.

There was silence as they ate then Carson suddenly stopped eating. "So," he said across the table, "Emily. My father told me you were busy accomplishing things."

Emily nodded, chewing. "I have."

"I just needed to be sure." Carson turned back toward his mashed potatoes.

My eyelids got heavy. This was getting boring. When I almost couldn't bear it any longer, Mrs. Sesmore whispered for all servants to head to their dormitories. Once in my bed, I propped myself up against my pillow and watched everybody do stuff before bed.

"You guys are horrible," Nathan said, picking at his hair. "*Who's* you," he mimicked. "The *bald* guy?" He picked up his pillow, laid down flat on his back, put his pillow on his face and screamed: "GOSH, GIRLS!" His body grew tense and then relaxed. Ari stood up on her bed.

"It's not our fault we don't know how things function around here," she cried.

"Exactly," I said, chiming in. "I bet you were just like us when you first came here."

Nathan removed the pillow from his face and rolled his eyes. Selene stretched on her mattress and touched her toes. "We need to do our rhyme before bed," she said, lying down and pulling the covers over her body.

Everyone got ready for bed. I was just about to nod off when Selene jumped up and did a little wiggle dance before screeching at the top of her lungs: "WE CAN DO IT!" Ari and I bolted up, and slowly shared a look. I could hear trumpets playing from rooms farther down the hall. A faint chorus from kids: "WE CAN DO IT!" Nathan sat up in bed. His voice was drowned out by everybody, but I still think he was singing. "WE CAN, WE CAN!"

When the show was over, Selene and Nathan laid back down in bed, exhausted. Ari and I remained in the same position we were in before. We finally relaxed and fell into bed. I hoped that we wouldn't have to do that every night. It would be too tiring.

I woke up. From what I could see on the clock, it was about 2:00 in the morning. We had gone to bed early, at around 6 or 7 o'clock, but I didn't care. Ari was not in the bed right next to me anymore. I shuddered and pinched myself. Maybe this was all a crazy dream.

I crept out of bed and the floor was cold against my bare feet. I stepped out of the room and there was a scream. I froze and craned my neck to see if I was busted.

There was a louder scream, and then loud sirens went off. Adults and kids rushed past me in sheets, stampeding, skidding, and jumping. One man managed to whack me in the face. A little girl tripped over my feet.

Everybody gathered on the main floor. A chandelier dangled dangerously above our heads. There was still no sign of Ari anywhere. We stood at attention. Emily came careening down the stairs, tumbling and tripping, her huge golden curls bouncing. She was in a flowing light pink nightgown.

She was gasping as loudly as Mrs. Sesmore. Finally, she swallowed and cried breathlessly: "There's-a-THING-in-my-my-room!" She finished off in petrified wailing. There was a little groan. Emily had seen a little insect and was probably going to make us exterminate it. Emily looked anxiously around. Somebody pounded me on the shoulder. I winced and looked around to see if it was Nathan. An aroma filled the air that surprisingly, wasn't unpleasant. A teenager sneezed in the background.

"Where's Ari?" I didn't know Nathan cared. I shrugged and tried to show a face full of concern and worry to match Nathan and Selene's.

"You're always supposed to come here when they call the alarms," Nathan said. "Order is *EVERYTHING* here."

"No kidding." I rolled my eyes.

Nathan stopped talking to me and crossed his arms. I turned my attention back to Emily. She was bouncing on her heels and biting her nails until Mistress Smith slapped them. That's when Emily flung her hands around in the air.

Carson suddenly appeared, looking flushed and tired. He was in the clothes that he had worn at dinner. He didn't even bother to change to go to bed. All the other servants at The Diamond Square were in pajamas that felt and looked like old brown tree branches. Carson shivered and was going to his room when Mr. Waite stopped him. He had just climbed down the stairs a second ago.

"Where have you been, son?" Another one of those questions that come out as statements.

"Outside, getting fresh air," Carson grumbled. "Can I go now? I need to think." Mr. Waite nodded slowly and instructed that I take care of the insect in Emily's room.

I angrily walked upstairs, opened and then slammed Emily's bedroom door, looking for anything. Suddenly, something moved in the distance. *Checkmate.* I looked around for protection and finally realized that the only weapons were my bare hands and a toilet scrubber in the bathroom. I chose option two and held the scrubber at arm's length. I heard another scuffle near the bed.

I approached it slowly. Suddenly, I screamed as something big and black came hurtling right at me!!!

CHAPTER 9

The Golden Bridge

It was impossible to sleep. It wasn't the fact that my bed felt like it was made from cardboard though. I kept shifting and rolling over and checking the clock which now read 1:35 AM. I quietly and carefully pried the blanket off me and rolled out of bed. The floor was freezing. I pushed the door open gently and Nathan turned over. I didn't even bother to see if he had woken up. I just stepped out and closed the door behind me.

The hallways and the stairs leading down to the huge main room were entirely dark. Goosebumps ran down my entire body from both fear and cold. I could barely see the guards blocking the entranceway. Ducking behind a potted plant, I could see the golden gates, tall as Goliath. It was breathtaking.

I saw a moonlit concrete path with stairs and decided to climb those instead. I went on all fours so nobody could see me. The concrete was rough.

I finally got a breath of fresh air. I was outside, and there was a tall fence with barbed wire. Tiny electrocution lines ran over it. Wow, this was more high-tech than I had expected.

But The Diamond Square didn't think of everything.

A pole was placed randomly near the fence. It was like those clotheslines that looked like a gray letter T. There was only one, and it was slanted and lonely. Two Ts were on the other side of the yard.

I scaled the slanted T, hopped over the fence, and then ran for I don't know how long. Then, I stopped and stared.

There was a little shopping plaza about a mile ahead of The Diamond Square. Shopping malls, mannequins, and cars surrounded me. There were even buildings. This was extraordinary. The most amazing sight was a lighted bridge. It had a glass bottom and golden poles that held golden bead-shaped lights.

A strange desire filled me.

I grabbed onto a building's roof that was standing firmly in the wind and used it to pry myself up. Now I was on top of the building. A cold gust of wind flew past me, and suddenly I knew what I was doing.

I jumped from building to building, catching on to whatever I could, like roofs and posts. Finally, I was on top of a porch that was level with the bridge. I walked past the golden railings, and the golden beads, and sat in the middle of all the beauty. I couldn't picture myself going back to The Diamond Square anytime soon. In fact, what if I just left completely? Nobody would come this far into a shopping plaza just to find one little girl, right?

Then my mind flashed back to Kris. My body relaxed with disappointment. I couldn't leave her behind! It would haunt me for the rest of my life. But if I did this just now, surely, I could do it again? Maybe tomorrow we could escape and show Nathan and Selene how it was done.

Just as I was thinking this, I heard footsteps growing louder and louder, but I ignored them. I looked down through the glass and saw cars and a few people and ignored the steps until they seemed to be right behind me. Shakily, I turned my head around and expected to see an army of guards, ready to drag me away from my paradise.

Instead, I saw Carson, his blonde hair shining almost white in the moonlight. My hands began to get sweaty and trembled slightly. I glanced desperately down at the glass bottom and wished madly that I could crash right through it. Carson raised his eyebrows and I realized this was the end.

"H…how did you get here?" I stammered, hoping to stall for time. Why hadn't the earth swallowed me up already?

"I took the easy way," Carson replied.

"*You* can climb buildings *too*?" I cried in awe. I put my hand to my forehead.

"What? NO! I took the stairs you idiot!" He kicked the glass bottom as if there was dust there. I dropped my hands from my forehead. Ignoring the insult, I tried to marry what he said with what he meant.

"There are *STAIRS*!" I yelled, flabbergasted. Carson rolled his eyes. I scaled half of the buildings in this huge plaza which was probably more than a plaza considering the size…AND THERE WERE STAIRS?

Carson kneeled and surveyed the earth below as well. He seemed just as intrigued as I was. "So, I guess you know why I'm here."

My heart began to beat. This was the moment where I would be locked up without anything to eat for a month. This was more like the moment where I would find my brain and run for my life without Kris. What am I thinking? I can't possibly leave Kris! I looked Carson right in his hair since he wasn't showing me his eyes yet. I wondered what I should say to him. *Your father isn't bald. He has a healthy head of hair. I meant to say Mistress Smith was bald. WHAT? I never said your father was bald!! That's ridiculous!!!*

Carson's blue eyes were dancing as he looked at me. His stern face dissolved into laughter. I wondered if this was a trick. He'll pretend to think it's funny, then he'll reach out, grab me, and stuff me into Diamond Square's dungeon, if they have one, that is. They'll put me into a pot full of soup and then I'll have a delicious end. The thought of soup, especially meaty human soup, made my mouth water.

"You're absolutely right," he cried. Then suddenly he stopped laughing and looked me in the eye. "I thought I'd never see the day a servant would tell him that."

I gulped. "No human soup then?" Carson looked at me like I had morphed into a glass cup. He shook his head. *No meaty soup then.* I sure worry about weird things nowadays.

Carson looked at the moon. "The moon's great, isn't it?" he exclaimed. "I never got to see it this way."

I gasped. "But you live here now," I protested, "how can you never see it?"

Carson shrugged. Then he got up and began walking towards the edge of the bridge. Stretching my eye limit, I saw gray stairs leading down to ground level. Mostly everything I've seen since I got here is gray with a few specks of color here and there. I decided to sit there.

"See you around." His voice sounded far away, but I didn't turn around to say goodbye or even see where he was. Before I could hear steps going downstairs, I heard loud alarms and sirens going off. I didn't know how far I was from The Diamond Square anymore, but that sounded like a fire alarm. Or maybe it was a smoke detector. What alarm or siren could make that much noise? Or maybe it was an Attendance Alarm because they noticed I was missing. A cold breeze fluttered by, and I got chills for so many more reasons than that.

"Sounds like the Emergency Alarm," Carson stated. "They usually call that for stupid reasons."

I relaxed a little bit. Carson suddenly held on to the golden railing and looked down. Then he froze. When I was about to ask if he had a fear of heights, he instructed me: "Look at this dude." I looked down with Carson and saw a man dressed in black. He stayed clear of cars and people and hid in the shadows.

"Shady." I stopped looking at him as Carson nodded his head in agreement. I looked down at the glass bridge and felt a little fearful as I saw the man walk back and forth. He paced back and forth until another man, dressed just like him, appeared. I kneeled on the glass bottom and pressed my face against the glass. They were both wearing hats, so I couldn't see their hairstyles, which really would've helped a lot.

Carson kneeled down too. The two men talked to each other in a heated, brief discussion. Then they departed in opposite directions. My heart felt heavy.

Carson stood up. "I better be going," he said. "My father will definitely be expecting me."

He headed down the stairs. I watched him, wondering if maybe I should follow him back to The Diamond Square. After all, getting caught would be unbearable.

After a few more minutes of wondering how I got to The Diamond Square, and debating who really was to blame for our life being destroyed, I started heading back. Everybody, including the guards were gone except the ones who guarded the tall golden gate. I slipped past them and went to the dorm. I was surprised to find Emily pale and shivering under my covers.

"When did you get here?" I squealed.

"A huge black spider is in my room!" Emily exclaimed. "I can't possibly go back there! Where were *you*?"

"Enjoying…the amazing…scenery?" It was the dumbest half-lie I'd ever come up with. I needed to make her think we were close. "We could hear the alarm loud and clear."

"You could've heard the alarm from England!" I wondered how far England was from here. Wherever this place was.

I shrugged. Emily got out of bed, froze, and looked at me. She informed me that Kris was in her room dealing with the monster and she was staying in her bed for the remainder of the night.

"This is *my* bed," I said. "You can put your princess curls on Kris's bed. 'Night."

Emily got up, lay down on the bed next to mine and kept up the awkward silence. I sat up on the mattress, aching for sleep. For the second time that night, I got up. I tiptoed to Emily's room. I didn't know where it was, but I could hear muffled angry mumbling and scuffling near the door, and I decided to peek inside.

I felt paranoid that it might be Mrs. Sesmore, Mr. Waite or even Carson but I peered inside. Kris was looking under the bed, not in a drawer, nope, she was looking right at me now.

I jumped back a bit. "Hi," I said.

Kris squinted at me. "What are you doing here?" she asked. "Uh," I stammered. "Girl, this place is haunted by a crazy huge black thing. You better leave while you can."

"You mean a little daddy-long-legs is dropping by around here and you're scared?" I leaned against the doorway casually and looked around, trying to appear nonchalant.

Kris shook her head. "This isn't a spider, Ari. This thing is the size of a *beaver*!" She held her arms out wide. "It has a mouth bigger than anything you can imagine. It'll probably be in the next folk tale."

"Mmm." I decided to go. Kris stopped me. "Aren't you going to stay?" I shook my head no. I had had enough excitement for one night as it was. There was no need to have my leg bitten off as well.

I walked down the hallway, and slipped into bed, ignoring Kris's shrieks and screams. My eyelids grew heavier, and I snuggled my nose into the uncomfortable pillow.

"ALL SERVANTS MEET IN THE DINING HALL," a loudspeaker a bit muffled by the closed door screamed. "I REPEAT, ALL SERVANTS MEET IN THE DINING HALL!" Selene rolled over and yawned while Nathan made his bed. I looked over to the bed on my right and was surprised to see Kris slowly beginning to sit up instead of Emily. They must have swapped spots. Something in my brain told me that Emily was probably the one to want to go back to her own room.

I got out of bed hesitantly and rubbed my eyes. There was breathing on the loudspeaker and a loud ring that made us all cover our ears. When it was over, we all went downstairs in our nighties to see what was going to happen.

Emily who had already changed, looked happy and refreshed. She bounced on her toes and wore a huge grin. Kris rolled her eyes, annoyed that she was in such a good mood. Everybody seemed a little grouchier too because of Emily's upbeat behavior.

I was probably the only one who saw the dark, purple bags underneath Emily's eyes. She was the most exhausted one here, but everybody was tired.

"Alright," Mistress Smith announced. "We had a rather interrupted night there. But we should all be happy that our dear Emily is refreshed." Emily yawned widely and covered her mouth. Again, nobody seemed to notice but me. Mistress Smith continued: "Today is Wednesday, correct me if I'm wrong." Nobody corrected her. Another yawn from Emily.

"While me, Emily, Mister Waite and his son Carson have our breakfast I expect you servants will have a piece of toast." Emily nodded.

Everybody went to the lunchroom, which was really the breakfast, lunch, and dining room. We squeezed ourselves through the archway and sat down at different tables.

Kris and I sat at a table while Nathan and Selene occupied one which was near a window. Sunlight streamed on Selene's hair as she excitedly said how we were going to bathe in the falls. "What falls, girl?" Kris asked, poking a hole in her last tiny piece of toast. "It's like springs and they're hot. There's a little waterfall that pours into the spring that's always full of natural bubbles. Not like the bubble baths of course." Selene clasped her hands together. Nathan ripped off some bread and stated: "You have to stay away from Davis and Simon though."

"Why?" I asked, studying my milk. It looked contaminated, but I could always drink fresh spring water, right?

"They like to do their 'stuff' in there," Nathan informed us. "I…I had to learn that the hard way." He shuddered visibly as he spoke. "Oh." Chills went up my spine. Maybe I shouldn't drink the water in the spring after all.

Kris put her tray on the side. "Child…." Selene wiped away her milk mustache and asked: "How come you keep calling people children?" Kris shrugged. "What's wrong with it, girl? I mean, kids are children, children are kids, you know." Her voice kept getting fainter as she rambled on. Selene shook her head.

Nathan stood up with an empty plate and a plastic cup of milk, and the rest of us followed and put our remains either in a stinking trash can or a ginormous sink. We lined up near the archway, fighting other pushers, determined to be first. Selene and Nathan were a few people ahead of us, and I was right behind Kris.

The untidy line went outside through green and brown grass, and through the same fenced gate with barbed wire with a million locks. Mrs. Sesmore rushed behind us, gasping, and puffing, got out a little key and unlocked all the locks one by one. I saw her stick it back into her dress pocket. I looked at her intensely. I had a feeling that I might want to keep track of where she kept that hidden. Just in case. The first person in line, a man with black hair swung open the wire door, and an extremely tall boy in his late teens with curly, red hair literally tried to pummel a hole through his arm trying to get to the spring first. The man grabbed the boy by his rags, pushed him back in the line, and went slowly down a little hill. The people near the front fidgeted and were excited to go into the water.

When Kris and I got our turn to go, I stepped down the low hill carefully, trying not to slip. I went in slowly. The spring was just like the one at that park, bubbling and babbling, warm and refreshing. I found myself trying to enter as secretly as I could with nobody looking at my almost bare figure. When I got out, the rags I wore were now wet but clean.

Kris got out a few minutes after I did and we ran into Nathan and Selene, both grinning like million-dollar winners. "What is it?" Kris asked.

"Selene and I just thought you'd like to know there's a cave around here," Nathan said, still grinning.

"That's, like- the stupidest thing I've ever-" I said. Kris shushed me. "What she *means* is we'd love to see it!"

"Okay then," Nathan whispered slowly. "Follow us." He led us around the right side of the spring. There was a huge cave that was probably a mine. "Is it a mine?" I asked. Nathan shrugged.

"Possibly could be," Selene agreed.

The cave was dark with a few holes from the roof of it allowing some sunlight. It almost reminded me of the train station. We went farther and farther into the cave. There was no sign of any valuables, and I couldn't hear the splashing of people bathing themselves in the stream. The farther we went the more hesitant Selene and Nathan became. At least we weren't lost. If we wanted to turn back, we could always go in the opposite direction. As we went down, we heard loud gasping and laughing. My heart felt like it was skipping beats.

We stumbled across a man in a wooden chair. He had gray hair that was balding in the middle. He looked like he was shivering even though he was in baggy, long clothes. We, kids, stepped back, hesitantly.

The man looked at us slowly. He didn't look starved, or even hungry. In fact, he had a turkey sandwich in his filthy hands. He eyed us steadily.

We stayed silent.

The old man got up and screamed: "I'LL EAT YOU!" Kris, Selene and I screamed. Nathan yelped.

A large lizard crept by the old man's feet. He grabbed the lizard and squished it, then ripped it apart. Selene gagged. The old man walked over to a fire pit and threw the lizard inside. After a few seconds, he literally picked it up out of the firepit, rolled his hand around in some mud for a minute, and put the lizard in his mouth. He turned towards us and smiled with the lizard still stuck in his teeth. What a waste. He had a perfectly wonderful turkey sandwich, and he ate a lizard instead.

He sat back down in his chair, still slowly chewing the lizard. Selene edged toward the entrance of the cave that was extremely far away. The rest of us hurriedly followed. While we were making our exit, the man clapped his hands, leaned back in his chair, and laughed. He saw another lizard and threw it into his fire. I shuddered and ran after the others.

When we came into the sunlight once again, we realized that hardly anyone was still in the line for bathing. Most of the servants had gone back to the Square and were trying to figure out what their duties were. Nathan and I had to clean Emily's bathroom thoroughly. Pathetically enough, he was the only one in the entire world that I wanted to talk to.

"Isn't it weird we keep on getting chores to do together?" I asked as I began moving rugs out of the bathroom. The white rugs were furry, and I was tempted to have a nap on them.

"Not really. People who share dorms usually get assigned to do stuff together," Nathan replied, putting toothpaste and a toothbrush in a cup, and placing it on the tile outside the bathroom. I nodded and began tugging on the last white rug, but it wouldn't undo.

"Oh." I began tugging harder and harder, but it was like it was glued under the sink. "Can I have a little help?" Nathan put his hands on the opposite end of the rug and tried to pry it off, but it wouldn't budge. "It's stuck," he announced. "You think?" I asked.

Nathan walked out of the door and returned with a bucket of water and a mop. I thought the water was for the rug, but it was just to mop the floors. I gave the rug one last tug, and this time it came off, but in a bad way. Some of the little furry hairs on the rug attached to the area under the sink. I picked at the hairs for a few seconds but gave up eventually.

I decided to scrub the toilet since Nathan was already mopping up the floors. "Where were you last night, by the way?" Nathan asked, putting the mop back in the bucket. "I mean, did you try to run away?"

I shrugged. "Not really." My intention wasn't to run away, specifically because Kris wasn't with me.

Nathan splashed the mop onto the floor a little too hard. Water specks sprayed the beige pattern on the bottom tile on the wall. Mistress Smith inched the door open. "Your class has started," she said. "Go quickly. Emily will be with you." *Of course, she will. Emily can NEVER be forgotten.*

I followed Nathan out of the room. The classroom was a large room with rows of wooden desks and chairs placed together. I was a little surprised that they were together. Nathan sat next to Selene, and I sat between Kris and Selene.

A girl from another row began squashing her behind right next to Kris. "Do you mind if I stay here?" We all nodded slowly, and she got up with an exasperated sigh. She sat right next to another girl in the back of us who was beckoning wildly to her to sit down. They began whispering as if they'd known each other for ages, which they probably had.

Mrs. Sesmore, her hair in a bun and wearing a pink dress entered the room. She brushed off her dress and began searching for a piece of chalk. This class was like nothing I have ever been in. The kids were falling asleep and being awakened by Mrs. Sesmore's raging hand.

Two hours later, I went back to cleaning Emily's toilet with Nathan, my brain filled with things that I'd either known before or probably wouldn't know in a million lifetimes. I started picking at the hairs under the sink because I didn't know what else to do.

Finally, Nathan threw the toilet scrubber and cleaning materials in my hands. "Go clean the toilets and then we'll be done with our first task." "Our first task?" I groaned, ferociously scratching the toilet's insides. Nathan nodded. "We have to uproot weeds in the garden outside." Gardening, what an amazing thing to do.

Once I finished trying to catch any stained spots, I headed to the kitchen along with Nathan to check up on Selene and Kris. The hallways were still long, and the rooms were still huge, so I followed Nathan to the kitchen.

Kris and Selene's hands were halfway down the bubbly water. They were laughing and giggling. It wasn't a surprise they got along so well. Selene turned around and waved. "Hey guys!" she cried. Kris whipped her head around. "Ari," she said, taking my hand excitedly, "I'm telling you Selene is just…wow." I nodded. Selene sounded like a *really* cool person.

Kris walked back to the sink and grabbed a white plate. It had flowery edges and a brown design in the middle. Selene, who was talking to Nathan, automatically shot out a hand, grabbed the plate, and hugged it to her chest. "Don't mess with this!" she whispered loudly in an angry tone. "I mean, really, do you *want* to die?" Kris shook her head slowly. "Exactly," Selene said triumphantly, handing Kris the plate back. "Be careful with this. It's Mistress Smith's most prized possession!" Kris rolled her eyes and began washing the plate like it was any other.

Nathan and I decided to head to the garden to get our second task for the day done before lunch. "Wait," Selene exclaimed, "where are you two going?"

"To the garden," Nathan smiled. "We, the Speedy Gonzaleses, have already finished our *first* task. Isn't that neat?" Selene rolled her eyes and mumbled something good-naturedly. "C'mon Kristina," Selene pushed, "we got to catch up to the two Gonzaleses over there." She gestured towards Nathan and me. Nathan smirked and opened the kitchen door then closed it, completely leaving me behind. I quickly whipped open the door and called out: "See you at lunch!" I closed the door and hurried after Nathan.

At lunch, Kris didn't say much. Being sunburned and tired, I didn't really mind. After all, she *did* eat all of her cup of peas, but at The Diamond Square, who wouldn't? As Nathan and Selene started a conversation about hands, I followed Kris with an empty cup. "What's up?" I asked as she threw her empty cup into the huge sink. I did the same thing. "Girl," Kris said, coming to a stop. "I messed up."

I stared at her. "We always mess up," I informed her. "It's in our DNA." Kris shook her head repeatedly. "No! I did something soooo bad you won't be able to copy it! Girl, I am dead meat! I'm serious!"

I grinned and shook my head. What could she possibly do that was *that* bad? What was there to do anyway? Did she go back to that creepy old man who said he could eat us? I began to get chills at the thought of it. Maybe she made some human soup but that wasn't allowed here in The Diamond Square, so she panicked and poured it into Mrs. Sesmore's dress pockets.

"What did you do?" I asked. "I really did two things," said Kris. "But the second one was stupid, so I don't really care. The thing that matters is…" She took a deep breath and then continued. "I lost my bag of ashes." She drew in another deep breath. I squinched up my eyebrows. "I don't even know what that was about," I replied. "I never knew why you would pack a bag of ashes anyway. I'm not gonna understand why you would want that until you tell me why."

Kris smacked her forehead. "It was my boots, alright!" she exclaimed exasperatedly. I gave her a blank look. "You know," she told me, "The ones that lasted through all of school. The ones that I wore when we went on prank wars with Axel. The ones I wore when the girl stole money from hotel customers. The ones I wore when we were at school with Kasie. The ones I wore when we were Downtown, and we jogged and met the girl with the unicorn and did the maze and ate candy apples and all of that." I nodded. "My boots literally were what I wore during the events of my entire *life* and now you don't know what they even are anymore?"

"It's not that I don't remember," I said defensively. "It's just that, since the fire, time just feels like it has slowed down with all these events that are going on. You know what I mean?"

"Well, I happen to think life has been boring since we came here," Kris protested. "But you *need* to help me find my boot ashes. I'm broken without them." I guess Kris would be broken without them, so I told her I would help her search for them after we had dinner, if we had dinner, that is. Kris reluctantly agreed.

A bell that rang (there were so many bells here) reminded us that lunch was over, and we needed to go back to our chores for the day. Everybody groaned and sauntered to the trash can or the sink. Kris and Selene went to the dishwashing sink and watched everybody put more and more plates into it. They sighed and cupped their heads in their hands. Nathan and I laughed at them and walked around the kitchen twice just to mock them a little. They would *never* finish washing the dishes now!

"Hey," Selene muttered, eyeing us. "Don't you have to go somewhere else?"

"*Dear* friend, Speedy Gonzales has all the time in the world," I told her. Nathan agreed.

Another wave of people put their dishes in the sink. This time it was only adults. The kids had already gone to do whatever they had to do. Nathan and I leaned against the counter and watched the crowd pushing through.

Finally, we decided to leave to go back to the garden. Wiping a bead of sweat from my brow, I was about to throw another weed into the rusty red wagon until I saw something in the grass. The dust on the ground picked up and wafted around me as I kneeled to inspect it. A grass snake swirled gently around in the grass and dirt.

When I was six, I used to feed and nurse those snakes. My dad was fine with it. My mom, not so much. I almost cried at the memory of the laughs we had when one snake made it inside and curled contentedly on the couch. I carefully allowed the snake to coil around my arm. My eyes brightened and I stifled a laugh as the thought of the most perfect prank to pull on Mrs. Sesmore formed in my head.

CHAPTER 10

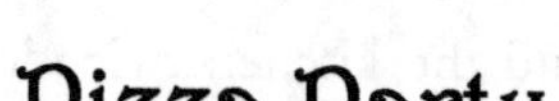

Pizza Party

I never knew people were such slobs. Some of these dishes were filthy, especially the one I was washing right now. I added a few extra drops of Joy and used the rectangular sponge to wash it clean. We had the worst job to do in this entire Diamond Square, especially since it was right after lunch.

I carefully deposited some broken pieces of plate in a basket, especially because Selene was moving a little closer to grab a cloth from my side of the counter. I shifted from one foot to the other and yawned. Carson suddenly strutted into the archway. Selene frowned and I felt a groan creeping up my throat. We both stopped scrubbing.

Carson casually walked over and took a plate from the black rack. He slid his index finger down over it, probably checking for dirt. When he saw nothing on his fingers, he shoved his hands in his pockets. "You two did a surprisingly good job," he commented. He shifted his gaze to me. "Aren't you one of that girl's friends?" he asked me.

"Oh, you have to be *kidding* me. There must be like, a hundred thousand girls here!" I cried. Carson crossed his arms. "You know, looks like you, curly hair, about your height, hanging around with you, and some other kids." He peered over at Selene and pointed at her as well. "You mean Ari?" I asked hesitantly. "What do you want with her?" Selene gasped, but when I turned to look at her, she was hiding her face with her hand. "What's going on?" I asked exasperatedly. Carson shook his head but then peeped inside the basket and his eyes widened. "What did you…? Why would you…? HOW can you….!" I shrugged. Why in the world were people freaking out about a plate?

"I…" he mumbled after a while, still a little shocked. "I thought she had run away."

"Why would my sister run away without me?" I asked curiously. This might have a little something to do with why she wasn't there when the bell rang. I put on my thinking cap, determined to think like a detective.

"She's your *sister*?" he screamed. Then, he stopped to think. "Well to think about it," he muttered faintly. "The levels of stupidity…" I interrupted him angrily. "Boy, did you just call my sister and me stupid?" I got ready for a fight.

"No…." he murmured. "You guys aren't stupid… just… very… different." While Carson struggled to find words that described us, I went back to washing like Selene.

"You're gonna die for that," Carson warned me, pointing to the basket as he finally made his exit. "But the Smiths believe anything." Before I could ask him what he meant, he had passed through the archway and was gone.

Selene was scrubbing and not talking, a sure sign that she was not clueless like me. "You know something about this," I told her.

"About what?"

"You know what he wants to do with Ari. You know what he means. You know."

Selene shrugged with a small smile. Feeling intimidated, I checked inside the basket and saw the pieces of plate jellybean shaped. Surprisingly, Selene hadn't checked in there to see anything. I closed my eyes and put one of my hands on a broken piece of plate. I needed to warn Ari about Carson. Carson probably hated Ari because she called his father bald. He must hate me too since I broke a dish and asked who his father was. Carson was probably so surprised we were related because maybe he could get rid of us easier that way. I opened my eyes. I needed to run to the garden and tell Ari that Carson was going to do something to us, and we needed to sneak out, like, *tonight.*

"Kris, Kristina?" Selene put her hand on my arm. I opened my eyes. "Are you okay?" she asked worriedly. "What's wrong?" I stared at her, then threw the sponge in the sink. I take back what I said about life being boring here. This Diamond Square is full of mystery. "Are we ever going to finish all of this?" I asked in distress, holding my head. Selene scratched the back of her neck and shrugged. "If we take too long Mrs. Sesmore will show us our next task and this will be somebody else's problem," Selene said.

"So that means we can go really slow and soon we'll be able to stop doing this?" Selene nodded. I breathed a sigh of relief and began washing more plates. Every time I brought a plate up from the water, I stared at my wrinkled hands. Selene and I fell into a routine. Wash, Rinse, Dry, Rack. Wash, Rinse, Dry Rack. Wash, Rinse, Dry, Rack. We actually started humming and singing it to ourselves softly. "Wash, Rinse, Dry, Rack. Wash, Rinse, Dry, Rack. Wash, Rinse, Dry..." There was a scream and both Selene and I jumped, startled suddenly out of our little routine chant. Selene threw the towel in the sink, and I dropped the sponge on the floor. I followed Selene and exited the kitchen. The screaming and shrieking continued. We listened to the sound, hearing it get louder and louder. We stopped in the main room, where servants were gathering to see the marvelous sight.

There was a snake winding and twisting around Mrs. Sesmore's jellybean-shaped body. She was screaming and most of the servants (especially the younger ones and teenagers) were snickering at her. Ari and Nathan were at one end of the circle of servants. They were laughing their heads off. Selene was giggling and I couldn't help but shriek with laughter. Laughing, after all, is contagious. Soon everybody was howling at Mrs. Sesmore who groaned and moaned and shrieked with fright.

"GET THIS THING OFF ME THIS INSTANT!" Mrs. Sesmore wailed. "GET THE WRETCHED DEMON OFF!" A man put his arms underneath the snake, carried it to a window, opened it, and threw it out. Mrs. Sesmore sighed loudly and actually breathed again. Any laughs or snickers automatically stopped. Everybody stood at attention. Mrs. Sesmore panted and cleaned off her dress. Then she cleared her throat and announced: "Whoever got the bright idea to put this horrible creature on my body will *DIE!*" Everybody jumped back a little at the emphasis and force put on the last word. "I can't start to imagine who would *do* such a thing!" Mrs. Sesmore shook her finger at all of us. "The investigation starts tonight." She stared at the floor; her face red with humiliation. Everyone went back to their tasks still whispering and giggling. I held my breath as she walked towards Selene and me. "Are the dishes done yet?" she asked. I gasped. I thought she was asking about the broken plate and felt my life was at stake.

"We're not even close to being finished," Selene explained. We stood there holding hands. This was when she would assign someone else to finish the job. Mrs. Sesmore nodded. "I see," she murmured. Two teenage boys walked past. I recognized the red-headed one, but not the other. "Norman and Harold!" both boys' heads turned. "You two…I want you two to do the dishes." The boys groaned and headed down the hall.

"What do we do now?" I asked Mrs. Sesmore. "Check your list for your second task, silly!" she replied bluntly. Selene pulled out the crumpled, damp list. The next chore we had to do was dusting the main dining area seats and shelves. My shoulders slumped. We had already done something similar just yesterday. I reluctantly followed Selene into the main dining hall.

Emily, Mistress Smith, and Carson were just beginning to eat. No wonder, they had a feast. For lunch, they had tuna and turkey with peanut butter and jelly sandwiches. My mouth watered at the PB and J. When our parents were alive, we used to have picnics and always eat those sandwiches.

The three stared at Selene and me for a while but continued their delectable lunch after a few moments. "Anything interesting to do?" Emily asked Carson, who was wolfing down a tuna sandwich. "Nope," Carson replied, his mouth full. I sighed and began dusting a shelf that held a glass cup. Mrs. Smith suddenly stood up and announced: "I must get my special dish. I can't eat without it." Emily, Carson, Selene, and I watched her hurry off. I shrugged and began dusting the glass cup a bit more.

"What's up with her and that dish?" Carson asked Emily. Emily shrugged. "I don't know," she admitted. "Everybody has a prize possession. Person, place or thing."

Carson nodded. Though he said nothing, I could see in his eyes he couldn't agree more. Ari and I had lost our prized possession. Our home.

There was a scream. Carson and I knew it was from Mrs. Smith. We both knew why she had screamed but I was the only one to get a little scared. Maybe that plate was more loved than I thought. Selene and Emily, well, they had no idea what was going on. Emily joined the mob of servants running down the hall towards the sound. I heard one kid whisper to the next: "I hope it's Mrs. Sesmore freaking out about a snake again!" I reluctantly put down the glass and dragged my feet across the floor.

Carson imitated my slow-paced walk. "You're gonna die," he reminded me. "I know," I groaned. We walked to the kitchen, and the farther we went, the slower my pace got. Even Carson got to the kitchen before I did.

Mrs. Smith was standing tall, cradling the basket. "Who could have *done* this?!" she cried to the crowd. Mrs. Sesmore panted her way towards Mrs. Smith. "Mrs. Smith, if you don't mind," she said breathlessly, "Norman and Harold were in this kitchen last. They're probably the ones who are responsible for this terrible mishap."

Mrs. Smith didn't skip a beat. "AH-HAH!" she screamed. "Oh! You two are in *so* much trouble!" Norman and Harold put up their hands. "It wasn't us, ma'am," the red-headed one insisted. "It was already broken." He pointed to Selene and me. "They were in there before us, ask them what happened!"

"We didn't do anything!" Selene protested, "Right Kris?" I agreed weakly. Carson cleared his throat but didn't say anything. I nervously clasped my hands together and prayed that nobody would suspect me. "I believe that the same person who brought the snake in did this," a girl with braces remarked. "It's probably somebody ignorant who doesn't know how things are done here, Mrs. Sesmore and Mrs. Smith." Mrs. Smith snapped her fingers. "Of course!" she cried. She faced the crowd.

"I'm aware that something is going on," she announced. "And the person responsible for these mishaps will simply be beaten with a cane." A gasp went around, and I cringed. Is that even legal nowadays? What had we become? The crowd thinned out, and people, for the second time that day, went out the door and returned to their tasks.

Selene stopped me as we walked down the hall. "What was Norman talking about?" Selene demanded. I shrugged. "He's just trying to pass the blame off on us, girl." Selene looked down at the floor. "Well, what if he isn't?" she asked. "What if it was somebody else?"

"Uh-huh, who would do that?"

"You, of course." Selene crossed her arms. "I'm not stupid." I put my hand on my chest. "I'm offended," I sputtered. Selene scratched the back of her hand. "Let's just do our jobs and keep a low profile," Selene suggested. I nodded and we headed back to the main dining hall.

After all our chores were done, the whole Diamond Square gang (myself, Ari, Selene, and Nathan) huddled up in our dormitory, played dominoes and waited for the dinner bell. So far, Nathan was winning but for a guy like him, that's not very surprising.

"Kris was the one who broke Mrs. Smith's plate," Selene muttered as I put down a 4/2. Nathan raised his brows. "Ah," he replied as he rested a 2/2 next to mine, "domino." Ari picked up the domino that Nathan had just put down. "Yah," she said, flipping it over a couple of times before putting it back in its place, "domino indeed."

"I *meant* the domino effect," Nathan informed Ari. Everybody except Ari gave him a look. "*This* girl," Nathan nudged Ari, "was the one who gave Mrs. Sesmore a friendly visit with the snake." We all burst out laughing.

"The domino effect is when one thing causes another thing to happen." This kid would have been one of the nerds at our school.

Just as Nathan was about to win by putting down his last black and white domino, the dinner bell rang. Nathan groaned as we automatically got up and started out of the door. Life can be so unfair sometimes. Life's unfairness is probably why we're here in The Diamond Square in the first place. I opened the door and followed everybody out of it. I closed the door behind me as everybody else headed down the hall.

Dinner, for me and Ari, was lightning quick. We needed to search for my boots. I barely looked down or tasted what I was eating, but I think it was cheese and…just cheese. Cheese and a choice of either milk or water. I chose more milk, while Ari chose water. Why that girl is obsessed with so much water is beyond me.

After swallowing a cheese block and swishing down milk, I got up with my tray and announced: "Finished!" Everybody else looked up at me, still picking at their cheese and milk or water. I eyed Ari. "C'mon," I pressed, "you're finished." Ari stood up reluctantly with her tray. She had finished her food as well.

We dumped any leftovers in the trash, put our plates in the sink and hurried out of the archway. As we headed toward the main room, I decided to tell Ari all about Carson and his weird behavior and that this situation probably wasn't safe.

"I need to tell you something, girl," I said, stepping carefully on the expensive-looking tile.

"What?" she asked.

"It's about Carson. He's really strange," I told her, forming every word carefully. Ari nodded like she agreed with me. "But Emily acted like a weirdo as well," she added. "She kept on stuttering and stammering like she couldn't believe her ears or whatever. But Carson's really nice." *I* couldn't believe *my* ears. "What in the world are you talking about, girl?" I asked. Ari shrugged. "I dunno," she admitted. "I mean, like, he's…like, you know.

Alright. Like a boy, I guess. You know, like…Drexel? Nice…but still a boy…"

I crossed my arms. "What do *you* know about Drexel?" Ari shrugged. I rolled my eyes. Forget my boot ashes, I needed to get to the bottom of this first! "You're saying Carson is nice when he's literally… a hater!"

Ari stopped walking, and so did I. "What are you talking about?" she asked. "He's kinda nice. *Kinda.*" I stamped my foot and sighed. Then I remembered Carson earlier today asking for Ari. What was going on with them? Was Ari making friends beside Nathan and Selene without me?

"Why is he nice to you and…ugh to me?" I asked softly, staring at my feet. Ari shrugged. I looked around the hallway and found a clock. It was **5:54 p.m.** "Let's just focus on finding my boot ashes," I murmured, beginning to walk down the hall. What in the world was Ari talking about? Why did she describe Carson as *nice?* She must mean, weird; extremely weird. I kept on walking down the hallway.

We didn't find my boot ashes. I looked out of the window while struggling to complete homework from The Diamond Square School earlier. This should seriously be illegal-- forcing you to do your homework when your mind just refuses to do it. If I'm not going to be a mathematician, a person who studies animals, or a scientist, why should I know the answer to all these questions? Why are these on different topics anyway? When I was a normal civilized teenager in actual clothes and went to an actual school, they didn't give us three pages of random questions about random subjects. But that's The Diamond Square for you. Hideously mysterious and weird. I still have some moments when I just can't believe I'm here, because this place is just…I can't even find a word to describe it.

"You've been staring out of the window for so long," Selene commented to Ari, "What are you even looking at?" Selene looked out of the same window Ari was staring out of. I sighed and twirled my pencil around my finger.

"The Diamond Square makes kids sad," Nathan said. "And not 'boo hoo' sad, but…sad." Ari rolled her eyes. "What would you guys do if I said there's an amazing plaza out there with pizza shops and a huge lighted bridge? You guys probably wouldn't even care but, whatever." Silence.

My brain, which had gone dead for a few minutes, suddenly sprang to life again and began comprehending the advantages of the things Ari had just mentioned. Everybody slowly stood up. "What are you saying, girl?" I asked. "Are you saying that we could go to this place you're talking about?

Ari nodded and grinned.

"We could have the best time of our entire *lives*," Selene exclaimed softly. Ari flung her arms around and nodded. "And we would be so happy because…" Nathan started. We all waited, but then Nathan, Selene and I chorused: "WE COULD EAT PIZZA!"

Ari smacked her forehead.

"But seriously girl," I told her, "We could branch out… and have fun…and eat *pizza*!" Ari sat down on the floor and looked like she was actually thinking about it. My mouth watered at the thought that pretty soon I could be sinking my teeth into delicious cheesy, pepperoni deliciousness. We all waited impatiently as Ari made her decision. Finally, Ari looked us all in the eye and nodded. We began cheering and dancing. I actually think Nathan broke out in a dance. I knew I was persuasive and knew we were going to have the time of our lives in that plaza!

The plan was formed in a group meeting. We would all go to sleep, wake up at one or two o'clock in the morning, sneak out, and be back fifteen minutes before the morning wake up bell was rung. It was approaching 6:30 and we needed to get some sleep. Nathan, who had a useful gift of waking up when he wanted to, would be the 'Wake-Up Call.' If we got caught, Selene would be 'The Stomach Victim.' While the rest of us hid somewhere, Selene would complain that she had a stomachache and wanted to go to the bathroom.

Ari would be 'The Searcher.' Ari said there was a leaning T that had been removed. I have no idea why she was talking about a leaning T. Well, Ari also said she knows that Mrs. Sesmore hides some keys that could help us escape from The Diamond Square in her dress pockets. Nathan and Selene knew the keys could open any lock, so we would split the keys. Selene and I would sneak out the bathroom window (I also have a bathroom excuse) while Ari and Nathan were going to escape from the gate. It was rather difficult to come up with this complex plan.

I slipped under my covers and closed my eyes.

"Rise and shine!" Nathan called softly, "All escapees wake up immediately!" I groaned and put my pillow over my head. "Five more minutes…" I whispered. I heard the movement of sheets and feet. Then Nathan literally shouted in my ear: "LET'S GO!" I jolted upright and stared outside the window. What in the world? Why was it nighttime? Was it daylight saving time already? As I rubbed my eyes, the plan hit me. The plaza, the fun, and the *pizza!* I hopped off of my bed and stretched. We all sat in a circle on the floor and whispered quietly.

"Ok, Selene," Ari said, "do your stomachache role" Selene put her hand to her forehead, closed her eyes and moaned softly: "Oh, my stomach hurts. I think I'm going to throw up. I need to use the bathroom. I…"

"Girl," I interrupted, "you sound like your lungs are being ripped in half. That's way too much." Selene dropped her hand and opened her eyes. "You guys said to make it believable," she complained. "What did you expect?"

"Believable perfection," Ari answered. She then turned to me. "Kris, while Selene is complaining, you're just going to slip to the bathroom, and Selene will meet you there."

I nodded. "I know." After a few more minutes of discussing, arguing, and planning, we all silently in single file went out the door.

The Diamond Square was black and gloomy. The floorboards were cold and hard. Something howled from a far distance. An owl hooted and the dark figure of a tree made me almost scream with fright.

I took a deep breath and wished us all good luck.

CHAPTER 11

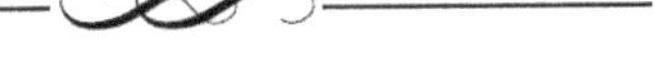

Caught!

The moon poured through the millions of windows in the building. Nathan and I waited at the top of the stairs as Selene went down them, holding her stomach. The Diamond Square was cold. Kris waited with Nathan and me. We watched Selene get stopped by one of the guards. The guard mumbled something we couldn't make out to Selene, and she groaned something in response. I almost sighed aloud. She had that same moaning 'end of the world' tune. Unless this guy was gullible, Selene had messed up our entire plan already.

"She has a stomachache," Nathan whispered angrily, "not a…not a…something that's worse than a stomachache!" He threw his hands in the air. "Tell me about it," I agreed. Surprisingly, the guard nodded and gestured towards the bathroom. "Beginner's luck," Kris murmured softly, as she crouched (hopefully unnoticed) against the wooden stairs.

Now that Kris and Selene were taken care of, Nathan and I had to venture to Mrs. Sesmore's room, and who knows where that is! I definitely should have thought that through. "So, where are we going?" Nathan asked. I froze. Ugh, the question I was fearing. I kept on crawling and acted as if I knew where we were heading. The doors looked identical. There weren't even any numbers on them or anything.

"Where are we?" Nathan asked again, as the hallway seemed to alter. Instead of plain, brown wood doors the doors were white. Tile replaced wooden planks and potted plants began appearing.

Again, I ignored him.

"Please tell me you know where this is," Nathan pleaded. I suddenly stopped. "Hey," I said, "shouldn't *you* know where Mrs. Sesmore's room is?" Nathan shrugged. "I'll try to figure it out."

It only took about five minutes for Nathan to figure out which door was Mrs. Sesmore's. I wasn't surprised. We used the keys to sneak out of the gates and met Kris and Selene a little bit past The Diamond Square, sitting in the grass. "What took you guys so long?" Selene asked, as they got up.

"A bit of stalling," Nathan explained, then turned to me. "Where's the pizza?" I shook my head and tried to think if he meant to say 'plaza' and not pizza. Why do they want that so much anyway? How long have they not tried it? Maybe for years…that's sad.

We all jogged faster the second I told them it was about a mile away. Or was it the fact that it had begun to spray? We started running as the rain slowly began to get harder.

We made it under one of the buildings' roofs just in time to get out of the way of the hardest rain I've ever seen. The water literally gushed past our bare feet and went into the drains as we went along the concrete path.

We had walked for about two minutes when Selene screamed: "PIZZA!" We all stopped. A delicious smell was wafting past us, and a few steps ahead of us there was a store with light pouring out of the windows. There was a pizza sticker on the glass door. As Nathan started pushing against the heavy glass door, my face darkened. Do you know how sometimes in animation they have an actual shadow pass across the person's face? That's how I felt just then. We hadn't thought everything through.

"Nathan…wait," I stammered, as he finally pushed the door open. He stopped and slipped in the water on the concrete. "What is it?" he snapped, getting back up. The smell of hot pizza fresh from the oven made me feel faint. "We…" The words were so hard to get out. "We…don't have any money." Everybody went silent. I bit my lip. Even I was starting to want pizza.

A little jazz band was playing near the building where we were. They were black men and reminded me of my family members. They had a hat on the ground to encourage people to drop money in it. Even from a distance you could see all the sparkling coins shining from the rain. They had stuffed the dollar bills in their pockets. They finished off a song and began gesturing toward a tiny pharmacy across the street. They began running there quickly.

Nathan grinned like a villain and approached the hat slowly after the jazz band had flung open the door and disappeared inside. "Boy," Kris said, "what do you think you're doing?" Nathan took a few more steps and didn't reply. "Nathan…" I warned, "Don't…don't you dare."

Nathan looked in the window to make sure the dough-flipping guy behind the counter wasn't looking. Then Nathan grabbed two handfuls of coins, stuffed them into his fragile, dirty, wet pockets, and stuffed two more handfuls in them. "There we go," Nathan said, "fresh coins for the occasion." He looked at us. "Well, what are you guys looking at? Come on, let's eat!"

Selene shook her head as Nathan pushed open the door for all of us. The dough-flipping man put the dough down and asked: "Well, what do we have here? Kiddies, I suppose?"

"One pizza please," Nathan instructed as he began pouring coins onto the counter, "eight slices, we'll eat two each."

"This store closes in 10 minutes," roared a janitor, mopping the tiled floor, "Can you really help them?"

The chef rubbed his chin. "Well…" he began. "You wouldn't shoo away children, would you?" Selene asked anxiously, staring up at him. "Yeah, and such paying ones too," I added, gesturing toward the pile of coins Nathan had on the counter. "That's just messed up," Nathan sneered, putting the coins back into his pockets. Kris stopped him and scooted them back onto the counter. "I want pizza!" she cried, "I want pizza!" We began chanting at the same time: "We want pizza! We want pizza! We want pizza! We want…"

The janitor headed back into a hall, sighing, and shaking his head. The chef shushed us. "Okay, okay! I'll give you pizza! Mama Mia!" He shook his head and went into the kitchen.

He must have had a pizza already prepared because just as we found a four-seater table to sit at, he brought it out and placed it gently on the table along with plastic plates and napkins. It was hot and steaming, and that just made it better. We all grabbed two slices and were only on the second bite when the bell on the door rang.

For a millisecond I thought it was just another late-night customer desperate for pizza like us, but my brain told me to turn around. There, to our horror, Mr. Waite, Mrs. Sesmore and Carson were standing right behind us. The pizza dropped from our hands.

"GET UP!" Mr. Waite roared. The janitor emerged from the hallway to see what was happening. The chef stopped flipping his pizza dough. We all stood up, our pizzas either on our napkins or in the pizza box. "Disgusting rats," Mrs. Sesmore commented, "they're supposed to be sleeping and we find them here in…what is this miserable place…*DOMINO'S?*"

"Actually," Selene began, "this isn't…" Mr. Waite stamped his foot. The chef jumped and squealed, dropping his pizza bread dough on the floor. "Do not speak," Mr. Waite said, "come with us immediately."

We all forlornly followed Carson, Mr. Waite, and Mrs. Sesmore out of the door. The jazz band had returned and were looking confused and scratching their heads. They were looking for their money. One of the men ran up to us and asked "Excuse me, but have you seen any money? In a hat? Like a Mexican hat? Or a sombrero? You know those…"

"How did you pay for the pizza?" Mr. Waite stated instead of asking. We all shrugged. "HOW DID YOU PAY FOR THE PIZZA?" Mr. Waite shouted. Nathan jumped and squeaked out: "Perhaps I may have borrowed some money?" Mr. Waite promptly pushed Nathan aside harshly and went inside the pizza store. Through the windows, we could see him putting the pizza box on the counter and shouting at the chef. The chef shakily returned all the coins and ran into the kitchen, clutching his hat with one hand. Poor guy.

Mr. Waite came out with the coins and gave them to the jazz band men. They jogged back out into the rain and found another place to set up and play their jazz.

Kris, Nathan, Selene, and I walked in the downpour, not even bothering to walk under roofs like Mr. Waite and Mrs. Sesmore and Carson did. We walked right on the roads, moving out of the way of the cars, and getting soaked in our rags until The Diamond Square came into sight once again.

I thought a reasonable punishment for our crimes was to send us to bed and to withhold breakfast. Instead, we were all crammed into Mrs. Sesmore's punishment office. It had a fan on the roof and wooden chairs. It would have been kind of nice if we weren't in such deep trouble.

Carson was sitting on a comfortable chair, between his father and Mrs. Sesmore. He hadn't said a word yet. "I am shocked, flabbergasted," Mrs. Sesmore announced. "I never knew servants who belong to *us* at The Diamond Square would sneak out and eat *pizza.*"

"Only Mrs. Sesmore is allowed to do that," Mr. Waite said harshly. Carson snickered and Mrs. Sesmore shot him a withering look. Carson looked at his lap, still smiling. Mr. Waite sat up straighter and said: "I do not even know what to say to you despicable kids. What do you have to say for yourselves?"

We didn't say anything. Would they even allow us to say anything? What could we say anyway? "I see," Mr. Waite continued. "Nothing to say. Hmm, what should we do then?"

"I think we should ban them from here. Toss em' out."

My body went limp. Selene began crying. Mrs. Sesmore screamed at her. My knees got weak. Everything spun around me, and my eyes burned. I barely heard Selene bawling and Kris joining in with her.

"Get up!" Mrs. Sesmore's voice rang out in my ears. "At 3:00 P.M. you shall go to the front door, and we will throw you into the streets. GET UP AND GO TO YOUR DORM!"

I don't know how but I managed to make it out of the room. Carson, Mr. Waite, and Mrs. Sesmore had stayed behind and had closed the door. None of our eyes were dry; even Nathan was crying. Why…out of the billions of people in the world…why did this have to happen to me? To Kris? Why?

Now I heard different voices. "*…Leads to your doom…*" "*Not every fairytale ends in 'happily ever after.'* I crossed my arms and walked, looking straight at the floor.

"This is all your fault, you know," Nathan informed me as we headed back to our room. "Me?" I practically screamed, "How is this *my* fault?"

"You're the one who told us about the pizza!" Selene snapped, obviously on Nathan's side. "ARE YOU STUPID?" I screeched so loudly that Selene took a step back. "*You* guys came up with the bright idea of going to the pizza place!" Nathan stood his ground. "What! You're upset you have nobody to pin this on, huh?" In fury, I clawed at him and slammed him into the wall. Never to be outdone, Nathan shoved me right back. We both jumped at each other but before things got ugly, Selene pulled me back and Kris hurried over to console Nathan. There was still a weird vibe between us all the way to our dorms.

(Kris and I were on the same team, Selene, and Nathan were on the other). Nathan opened the door, and we went inside changed into dry clothes and snuggled under our blankets. The tears I wanted to cry were still stuffed up inside me. I closed my eyes.

I rolled over and blinked. Sunlight was peeking through the windows and shining on our beds. Kris was waking up and she was stretching. I rubbed my eyes and checked the clock. It was 9:32 AM. I squinched my eyebrows in confusion. Why hadn't we eaten breakfast yet or started our chores?

"Finally," Nathan began, "you two are awake. *Finally.* You guys are very heavy sleepers. I mean, you slept through the morning bell!" Selene made her bed while Nathan was talking. "I don't even know why I'm doing this," she commented, "It's not like I'm going to sleep in it tonight or something."

What happened a few hours ago during the night instantly came back. Kris and I flopped in our beds at the same time. I think it's a sister thing, but I don't know. I covered my face with my pillow. I heard Nathan's muffled voice: "Wow Selene, way to darken the mood."

After a few minutes, Nathan announced: "Ok, let's go guys. I think we can catch a few scrap pieces of breakfast in the kitchen." I took the pillow from my face. "You want us to get in *more* trouble?" I shrieked. "I'm not going," Kris protested, "go away."

"Well, we're already gonna be kicked out of this place today," Nathan reasoned with us, "It's not like we can get in any *more* trouble than we already are in, right?" I had to admit, he had a point. It's not like they could do anything worse to us, right? We could simply do anything we wanted to. We could even try and go back to that plaza.

"You've got a point," Kris said slowly, "I guess I'm in." I nodded too. I leapt off my bed, and with Nathan, Selene, and Kris we walked into the hallway, grinning widely.

The hallway kids almost made me lose my grin. They were acting so sympathetically. A guy patted Nathan on the back and said: "You were a good man. Rest in peace." And another girl literally hugged Selene and cried: "Thank you so much for teaching me how to do bird origami! I'll never forget you Selene, you little angel!" Selene hugged her back, giving us a weird look.

We made it to the kitchen and found some leftover gravy-covered peas and ate them gladly. I told everybody about going back out to the plaza for lunch, and they slowly agreed.

When it was one hour, thirty-eight minutes and two seconds until we were supposed to go to the Punishment Room, my heart began beating harder and faster, and there had to be a whole colony of butterflies in my stomach (if butterflies are in colonies, that is, which they probably aren't). Kris hadn't said 'girl' or 'child' for a while now, a sure sign she was just as anxious as I was.

When it was finally 3:00 P.M., we all went out of our dormitory and down the hallway towards the Punishment Room. There were flyers all around The Diamond Square, announcing what was going to happen to us, and since morning they had increased in number. Even more people were saying their goodbyes to Nathan and Selene.

Nathan wasn't Mr. Happy Fun-time anymore, especially as we approached the door. He finally growled at me: "I can't believe I'm going to either die or be kicked out of here. And all because of two ignorant girls."

"Like it's our fault this is happening."

"My goodness, it *is* you and Kris's fault!"

"No, it's not!" I snapped with my hands on my hips. "*Everything* in my life is falling apart since you and your sister came!" Nathan cried. "I had to share me and Selene's once-roomy dorm with you guys! Then you both did mischievous things that probably got Mr. Waite and Mrs. Sesmore angry. Now we're caught doing something horrible and guess who also gets blamed? Selene and me." He crossed his arms and turned away from me.

"Nathan," I began, "Life is...unpredictable...I should know because..." Nathan interrupted me and said coldly: "You don't know anything about life and how it works." I blinked at the rudeness of his tone. How dare he!

"For your information," I refuted him, "I *do* know how life works.

Kris and I…our parents died when we were only seven! *Seven!* Then we lived with our Aunt Maybelle until we were twelve, which is when we worked at the Moody Moon Hotel. When we turned 13 a couple of months ago Aunt Maybelle allowed us to have our own suite in her apartment. It took me a moment to continue. "When our apartment caught fire…we got a call by some stranger…we still don't know who he was…we got kicked onto the streets…so I got the idea of coming here." I stopped, for one, because that was the end and two, there were so many unsolved mysteries in my life. I had to figure them all out.

"Heartwarming story," Nathan said, "but you two still don't and will never belong here." He began to catch up with Selene and Kris and declared coldly, just to me: "You two would have been better off in the streets."

My head was still reeling from Nathan's awful words. When we arrived at the Punishment Room's door we sat down on the floor. Minutes passed. Nobody opened the door and beckoned us inside. I told Kris all that Nathan said. "He's just jealous of us, girl," she announced, "don't listen to him."

After an hour, Carson walked by and asked: "What're you guys doing here? You were given a pardon earlier today." Then he walked away with a stack of papers in his hands.

I blinked. We all blinked. I blinked again; I had nothing else to do but blink. Nathan hopped to his feet. "Let's go before he says it's a prank," he whispered, running down the hall. Selene followed him. Kris was right behind Selene. Literally, I was the only one walking a confused, slow walk, glancing back at Carson until he had turned a corner and was gone.

The bridge's glass was cold against my legs and hands, but I continued stargazing. Some people might think I was crazy. *You just got pardoned from a serious punishment and you're doing wrong again?* Well, it's not *my* fault this place is too pretty to never ever see again. Besides, I had never seen the moon like this at The Diamond Square. When we were still in our apartment, looking out the window back then it looked like a little white circle. Now, here, I can see all the craters, it looks way bigger, for sure, and it's just so marvelous…so extraordinary.

"Well, well, well, look who decided to come back," a voice said. My heart thudded. I turned around and saw Carson. How did he get here? Did he follow me again like last time? "Um…" I forced a smile. "How did you get here?"

Carson didn't answer. He was still looking through the glass bottom of the bridge. "Is it me…" he said quietly, "and are these the same dudes we saw the other night?" I peered through the glass, and saw that Carson was right. The two suspicious men were back, talking and waving their hands in the air like they were on fire.

"Maybe we should call the police," Carson suggested, "they don't look like they're up to any good." I snorted. "What if they're friends?" I asked, "who like black…a lot…and fight…a lot…but can still be friends…"

By the look on Carson's face, I knew he really wanted to say something offensive but couldn't make out the words. "Whatever," I said, "we can call the police." Carson nodded, and I got up. We walked down the gray staircase and came to a room I'd never seen before. It was gray, had a little desk, like a help desk, and a phone booth in a corner. I could hear the men's voices now, so while Carson began calling the police. I hid behind a bush and listened to them.

"Where are they?" Voice Number 1 asked.

"We had them covered," Voice Number 2 answered, "honestly, I'm telling ya. Scurried away." Silence, then: "Sorry, but if boss wants the rats, then I have to give him the rats." Voice Number 1 seemed angry. "How hard is it to cage a couple of rats?" he shrieked. Rats? Who wanted to cage rats?

"Whatever," Voice Number 2 snarled, "I'll catch you later." Voice Number 1 called after him: "Catch! Catching them is way better!" I saw

Carson looking around and I hurried toward him. Breathlessly, I exclaimed: "They're talking about rats!" Carson looked at me. "What?" he asked.

"Rats!" I blurted, "the two shady men were talking about rats, and how they already had them covered, but they had to listen to the boss because the boss wanted the rats and the other one wanted the rats caged again for some weird reason, because who wants caged rats? I mean, no one *wants* rabies!"

This wasn't going to be good. Carson shook his head. "We called the police to tell them 'Oh hey, we called you because two men want caged rats?' Do you know how stupid we would look?" I squeezed my lips together. "True," I murmured, "Are they taking them to the police station?" Carson nodded.

Forty-five minutes later, I was sitting down in a chocolate brown cushiony chair, right next to Carson. The chief was sitting with a jug of steaming coffee. "Well," he exclaimed, "what seems to be the problem here?"

"My pal here will explain everything," Carson smiled. "Uh..." I stammered, "well...There are these two men...and uh...we've seen them before...well, you see...this is the second time we've seen them...same shady clothes...Well...this time I overheard them and well..." The chief began sipping his coffee. *Oh no,* I thought, *now he'll spit it all out.... on us.* "Well...." I continued, "They were saying stuff about...well...caged rats?" I squeezed my palms together.

He did not spit out his coffee. He swallowed it swiftly and put the mug down. "That's so, eh?" he asked. We nodded. "What time is it?" the chief roared, "the middle of the night? You called me in the middle of the night about some caged rats?" He stood up. "Go before you get yourself in problems, kids." He walked away with his coffee in his hand and slammed the door behind him.

I rolled over in my bed, blinked slowly and looked toward the open window exposing the sunlight and then at the clock that read 7:04 AM. I crawled out of my bed, crumpled the sheets into a ball on the mattress and headed out of the door.

They were still serving more peas and milk in the lunchroom, so I grabbed a bowl and sat at a different table than the others. I was weary and tired. Had I really gone to the police station or was that just a dream?

It's a dream, I thought. I wouldn't be dumb enough to go back on that bridge again, right? *Right,* I thought firmly as I went out of the archway, *right.*

CHAPTER 12

Whodunit?

Can somebody please tell me what is happening? Are we off the hook? We aren't gonna be kicked out? We aren't gonna die? Still, I went to bed furious and sad but woke up happy and refreshed. A little hungry…but nothing a little breakfast couldn't fix.

I practically skipped down the hallway past all the kids, groaning and sighing. I literally heard my favorite song playing over and over in my head, but this time I didn't get sick of it after the tenth round.

I didn't see Ari until breakfast was nearly over. She grabbed whatever was left and sat down at a table far away from us, looking cross and exhausted. I didn't wave her over, because something told me that she did not want to sit with us.

After a shower, I was back to normal. Nothing was so special about life. I dried off and went to my duties. Thankfully, this time I had a task to complete with Ari. Unfortunately, it was washing clothes and drying them. I liked chores because they kept us responsible. Ari may not have liked them as much as I did, but she hasn't complained since we got here.

"So…" Ari began, "what's going on?" I put the heavy white basket on the floor and clipped a brown shirt to the white clothesline. "Not much," I answered, "why don't *you* share something? You didn't sit with us at breakfast." Ari shrugged. "Can you believe we're off the hook?" Ari changed the subject. I shook my head. "They didn't come and knock on the door to say it was a joke either," I finished. "Weird." I bent down and put *another* brown shirt on a clip and clipped it onto the clothesline. "People came to our dorm last night?" Ari asked, folding a white shirt, "I didn't know that." Something suspicious was going on with this girl. "What do you mean you didn't know that?" I asked. But before Ari could answer, Mrs. Sesmore interrupted us and announced: "You're up."

"For what?" Ari and I asked in unison. Mrs. Sesmore opened the screen door which led to the inside and left it open. Ari went in and I closed it. "For testing, of course," Mrs. Sesmore exclaimed exasperatedly, leading us back to the Punishment Room. Ari and I were hesitant to step inside. I thought about running away but stepped inside anyway. Were we in trouble again?

"What are we going to be tested for?" Ari asked, being her usual curious self. "Mistress Smith and Emily will be leaving this night and Mistress Smith wants justice for her favorite and most treasured dish being broken. She wants to test everyone. And I mean *everyone*." Mrs. Sesmore sat down in a chair. Mr. Waite was also there, so were Emily and Carson. I avoided eye contact with Carson…and everybody else really.

"So," Mistress Smith said, beginning the already awkward conversation "where were you when the plate broke?" Ari, who liked to claim innocence, replied: "I was in the middle of the screen door. One whole move before pulling up my fifth weed. Slow progress you might be thinking. Why was I only on my fifth weed you may ask? Well…"

"We never asked," Mistress Smith interrupted, "but keep going. Go on now." Ari continued: "*Well*, I was going to answer your question 'why you may ask? 'And…" "Mistress Smith banged her fists on the table. "CHILD, FOR THE SAKE OF NEPTUNE," she roared, "NOBODY ASKED YOU THAT QUESTION!" Ari stared at her. "Let the child finish," Mr. Waite instructed sternly. Mistress Smith vaguely nodded. "*What* I *was* going to do was answer your question of…" I shook my head. "Don't act dumb," I whispered. Ari then said: "So…I was only pulling up my fifth weed because Mrs. Sesmore was screaming because a measly snake was on her. Then I continued to work when I heard *another* scream lasting for a full five minutes so I ran down the hall and traced all the screams and…" Mr. Waite gestured for Ari to stop blabbering. "What about you, ma'am?" Mistress Smith asked wearily, "Let us hear from you and then you two can go."

Mrs. Sesmore cleared her throat. "Remember, I also want justice for the little brat who put a snake in one of my drawers, that hopped right on top of me. Please do not cut into my time of investigation." Mistress Smith nodded. I realized that I was supposed to be talking. My heart skipped a beat. I was horrible at lying, which some people might think is a good trait but lying casually (like Ari) is something that can get people out of fixes like this.

While I searched for words, my hands became sweaty. I stammered, "um, well…wait…uh…" then I decided to stall for some time. "Um, what was the question you asked me again?" Ari looked at the floor. "The question was where were you when the plate was broken," Emily recited and flipped her beautiful blonde curls. She was wearing a white dress with matching white barrettes in her hair, white gloves with white pearl earrings and a white purse for her last few hours here. I sighed and timidly said: "Uh…well, I was maybe…seeing my next task…which um, well, was in the main food room…Ask Mistress Smith or Carson or Emily…you guys were all there…" Mistress Smith tapped her pen on the table. "I admit I did see you," Mistress Smith murmured, "but what was your last task before that?" My heart started beating faster. It stopped for what felt like a minute and was now beating harder and faster.

"Um…um, I dunno…can't remember…well…I think there are some di-ff-i-cu-l-ties with me remembering that." Mrs. Sesmore sighed. "Her last task was the kitchen," she informed Mistress Smith, "specifically…washing the dishes in the sink." I knew then I was in trouble. "That's not true!!! I exclaimed. All eyes in the room locked with mine. I shrank back into my seat. "Um, um, well," I squeaked, "what I mean is…um, I really don't think…um, or remember…that happening."

"Then we can check the records!" Mistress Smith exclaimed, getting to her feet. "Finally, this mystery is getting somewhere!" Mrs. Sesmore left the room to get the records. I gulped. "The records state what tasks servants did and at exactly what times," Mistress Smith said, smiling, "so now we'll know if Miss Kristina is lying or not." My eye twitched.

Two minutes later, Mrs. Sesmore puffed her way through the door. She grinned and presented the files to Mr. Waite. He read: "Miss Kristina…here, I see your name…dishes from…breakfast to after lunch…Then…the two boys…Mmm…"

I was known for not giving up, so I didn't. "Um, I think you should ask them because um…" My voice was very soft. "Um…because I believe there are some di-ff-i-cu-l-ties with your files…" I bit my lip nervously.

"The files are *never* wrong!" Emily exclaimed, flipping her light blonde curls again. Carson looked at her, and she sat down. "Yes," Mistress Smith replied, "they rarely…or ever are. So, Miss Kristina." She eyed me. "If you claim not to have broken my dish, what were you doing?"

"Um," I stuttered, "I…I was not in the kitchen for lunch. Uh, I had…um…gardening?" The moment I said it I instantly regretted it. Ari had just said she was in the garden. Uh-oh. "Interesting," Mr. Waite commented, "I thought Nathan, who was in here a few minutes ago, said he was in the garden with Miss Ari over here. So, Miss Ari, was Miss Kristina with you in the garden?" I looked at Ari, expecting her to say something smart to get us both out of this mess.

"Ummmm," Ari grunted, "uhhhhhh…" Mr. Waite tapped his watch impatiently. "Time is ticking," Mr. Waite reminded her. But Ari kept uhh-ing and umm-ing like this was the hardest question in the world. This was starting to get nerve-racking. Goodness knows what Ari might say!

Ari and I have a system where we can talk to each other in our own secret language. I think twins can do that, or when there is somebody who's really special to you and you know them well. *"Hurry up and give an answer!"* I roared at her, *"think of something smart to say, alright? Girl, you can't say 'yes' on the spot because all this hesitance will make them not believe us!"* Ari replied: *"Why'd you say garden, though? Of all the things…the garden? Why?"* I couldn't make out the rest. I could hear myself screaming at Ari: *"So I messed up, but at least I got this far! You're a people's person, so do something about this! Do you want to get in trouble AGAIN? Because, if you do, that ain't gonna get us nowhere."* Ari snapped at me: *"Don't put me under pressure! I can't function properly!"* Then, she communicated in a more reasonable tone, a 'think about it' tone. I only understood a few bits of what she was telling me. What I knew was that it wouldn't be so good for me. Something like: *"Look, how about you…And then I could try a plan…you won't…for long…I would never let something so…so, how about you think about it? I know it sounds…for you, but…okay? I just…"*

"When you two are done your little…I don't know what," Mr. Waite boomed, "we would still appreciate an answer." Ari gave me a small nod that was something like: *"Don't say anything. I have this all under control."* I shuddered. She gave everybody eye contact and then answered: "Kris was not with me and Nathan in the garden. I have no idea what you're even talking about."

"Whaddya *mean* you don't have any idea what they're talking about? Girl, if it weren't for Emily saying we need to think about this, I'd be cooked!" Ari and I walked down the hallway, back into the garden to clip up more clothes on the white clothesline.

"I thought we'd have a better chance of getting rid of this mess if…" Ari stopped, then continued: "If one of us has the problems and…one of us thinks of solutions." I glared at her, and Ari stared at the floor. "Sorry," she mumbled. "I know it wasn't very cool to ditch you like that, but our problems just would've gotten worse if we were both in them." I sighed. That was Ari, probably secretly having the ability to lie, but having so much sickening truthfulness that people have to cut her off with all the truth spilling from her mouth.

"So, what is your plan?" I asked as Ari opened the screen door that led outside. The sun hit me instantly. "Uh," Ari began, "well…it's more like a five-second plan…Not like a thought-through plan…"

I stared at her. "Do you mean you threw me under the bus for nothing?" Ari stamped her foot. "Not nothing!" she cried, "the sake of my *life* counts for something! We gotta keep at least *one* head above the water!" I rolled my eyes. "And, of course," I mumbled, "it has to be yours."

"Whaddya *mean* you don't have any idea what they're talking about?" Nathan laughed as he finished his slice of bread. "That's exactly what I said, boy!" I added, searching for crumbs on my plate. Selene came over, noticed Nathan laughing and asked: "What's going on, guys?"

"So, you'll never believe it," Nathan giggled while Selene sat down and began taking huge bites out of her slice of bread, "but, um, Kris and Ari were getting tested to see if they broke the plate, right? And nervous Kris messed up and said she was in the *garden*!" Selene almost spit out her bread. Nathan hooted. I crossed my arms. "Everybody makes mistakes!" I stated, "why is everybody making such a big deal out of what happened today?" Nathan waved me away. "Anyway," he continued, "Mr. Waite asked Ari if Kris was really in the garden, and can you guess what Ari said?" Selene guessed: "She…said no? She said…yes?" Selene took another huge bite. It was going to be gone in two more bites at that rate.

"She said 'nope!'" Nathan remarked, "and, guess what? She doesn't even have a plan to save Kris! And who needs help? Of course, the brainiac with the 300 IQ!" Nathan pointed to himself. "I never asked that!" Ari protested, "just because I…well, I *may* need some help to save this girl's gut…but…I never said that…so…yeah." Ari took the last bite of her bread. I smiled, satisfied for some weird reason. Suddenly, I bolted up with happiness. "Wait!" I cried. Everybody at my table stared at me. "Emily and Mistress Smith are leaving today!" I observed happily.

"Oh, they are?" Selene asked, finishing off her bread. I nodded. For me, that meant less talk about the stupid dish. The end of lunch bell rang, and everyone packed up.

The magic has returned. God probably has been helping us lately. I should've been herded into another investigation, but it was canceled again. Of course, something is up but I don't really want to find out what it is.

We would watch Mistress Smith and Emily leave. They'd be leaving on a train. Mistress Smith eyed me *almost* the *entire* time as Emily announced what a wonderful and interesting trip they would have, blah, blah, blah. She went on and on and on about how excited she was about visiting again in the New Year. She jumped up and down at the thought. "On New Year's Day they eat cake and ice cream," Selene whispered to me.

On hearing Emily's announcement about visiting again early in the New Year Mistress Smith cocked her head and asked, "Are you really sure we can afford to come back at *that* time? I mean, January?"

"What's wrong with that?"

Mistress Smith sighed. "We promised Dick we'd be at his interview, TV show or whatever." She turned to Mr. Waite. "You do have cable here, don't you? Wouldn't some people like to see us?"

"We have a radio in the guest rooms," Carson offered.

"This ancient dump," Emily muttered.

"Anyway, we will *not* be coming back in January -attendance day," Mistress Smith confirmed, "so goodbye."

With that they walked out the door.

I had never been happier since I came here.

CHAPTER 13

━━━━ ∽ ━━━━

The Parade

The Diamond Square was the best in the fall. There would be orange, red, and yellow leaves, and even though I haven't done it since I was a kid, I couldn't resist jumping into them. It did get colder though, and the thin blankets never protected us enough. It was very cold during the night. The worst part about fall was that we had to run actual errands now. Diamond Square teens and adults had to go all the way to the plaza to collect letters for Mr. Waite (which I don't think he ever read) and select shoes and clothes for Mrs. Sesmore. Sometimes they would send us to the plaza for letters, for food, for clothes, and when we brought these items to them, they made us return them. What was the point of all this anyway? Of course, I haven't said that to anyone.

Fifteen servants have either been removed, thrown out the window or whatever. That's six kids, four tweens, three toddlers and two grown-ups.

The bridge at the plaza had been decorated with artificial fall leaves. There was even going to be a Fall Parade and some servants have been thinking of sneaking out and going. I haven't seen many parades in person and from what I've seen on TV, there's usually a bunch of instruments and people playing those instruments, so I don't think it's worth sneaking out to see that. But Nathan and Selene had this weird tradition where they attended one each year since they came here.

Why couldn't Nathan and Selene figure out that this was a horrible idea? Sure, I snuck down to the bridge a couple of times…but that was when nobody was around! Parades are nice and crowded with nosy people, but of course, Kris was on board with the idea. 'What could go wrong since we have magic on our side?' she quoted. That's what we called it. Since the very first time we got in trouble, nothing happened but that was no reason to go ahead and push luck. I mean, what if the magic was sick of us or something like that…

Am I the only person who thinks this idea is stupid?

"Okay, we're going to use the Sesmore solution to answer this equation," Mrs. Sesmore instructed, pointing to the blackboard with her chalk. "So, first we have to…Benjamin, Maxwell…quiet, please…Oh okay." Mrs. Sesmore stopped writing to face us. "I'll wait, short one at the back. OKAY! Daphne NO DINNER! ***SILENCE*** BOYS!" She tapped the chalk against the blackboard again in agony.

"My favorite person in the band is that lady with a head shaped like an adorable red M&M," Selene informed us. We were all still talking about the Fall Parade.

"You have to be kidding me," Nathan whispered loudly, "She's basically the definition of scrappy junk."

"I thought our clothes were the definition of that," I said bluntly. Nathan shrugged. He had also declared that a few days ago.

"And then we're going to add this and multiply this…" Mrs. Sesmore's voice rang out. She had been a helter-skelter teacher so far, teaching us a different subject every half hour. Right now, we were doing math, our last subject until we had chores again. Today I got to clean the main dining hall with some other person I'd never seen or heard of before.

"Poppy Parrot is the guy who gives out delicious ribs to some people who attend the parade," Nathan stated.

"Who gives out ribs to people?" I asked.

"Poppy Parrot does," Nathan replied.

"Our mother used to make some juicy ribs boy," Kris said, "I'd like to see if Poppy Parrot can do better."

I didn't want to see Poppy Parrot do anything!

I like striking up conversations with people I don't know to make extra friends, but something about my cleaning partner told me to shut up and just clean. She didn't look at me and cleaned really, really fast.

She didn't look like she was in a talking mood.

"So, did you hear about the parade?"

The girl shook her head.

"Did you know there *was* a parade?"

She nodded.

"Hey, can you talk?" I asked.

"Yes, I can talk."

"Oh, okay.

"Can we please just clean now?"

"Okay, then…"

We were finished in half an hour flat. We had worked in awkward silence punctuated only by the screeching, squeaking and spraying of cleaning. Our next task was to make sure all the windows in the main room of The Diamond Square weren't smudged. So that meant we had to clean the windows, inside and out. We got some spray for the windows and began scrubbing. I remember doing similar stuff to the sliding glass doors in Kris's and my apartment. It was freezing outside, and the glass windows kept frosting up no matter how hard we scrubbed, so that was a problem completely beyond our control.

After that, we had a chore where we had to take out the six bags of trash that were beginning to stink up a portion of the lunchroom. My buddy and I each took one bag and brought it outside to the main garbage.

Out here, I could see The Diamond Square, actually, for the first time. It was honestly a gray slab of rough concrete with dozens of windows and a gloomy greyish-reddish roof. And if the truth be told, on the first day here, that girl who looked like she was experiencing nausea while taking out the trash had been under-exaggerating because the trash smelled absolutely horrible.

The parade was scheduled to take place on October 18th. That day I awoke to the screeching of the Wake-Up bell and sat up slowly. The one calendar we had in a corner of our room sent my heart into a flutter. Today, we will see the parade.

"I heard the parade starts around 11:00 am," Nathan stated as soon as we were all up, "so we might want to save all of our plaza errands until that time…"

"Sounds good," said Selene, "when does it end?"

"I dunno," Nathan replied, "but I don't care when it ends, and I don't care if it breaks into lunch and people get suspicious. I'm not leaving until Poppy Parrot comes on and gives out ribs."

"How many ribs does he have?" Kris asked.

"You have to help him out to get a rib," Nathan answered.

"What do you mean help him out?"" I asked.

"If he sneezes say bless you! If a rib falls, catch it before five seconds are up and offer it to him!" Nathan cried. "He won't take it and you'll be able to eat it."

Walking down the hallway I grabbed Kris by the arm and secretly began talking to her. "Don't you see this is gonna end badly?" I inquired.

"What will go wrong?" Kris asked.

"What if somebody asks us about our parents and where they are or something like that?"

"We lie," Kris said bluntly, "and say, "Oh! Our parents are getting some food at the stands for us" or, "Oh! They're talking to a friend somewhere. They'll be back soon.""

"But parade people are so overprotective," I exclaimed, "they'll keep watching us, to make sure we're *not* lying. They'll report us to a nearby officer and the officer will make us say that we live at The Diamond Square!

Then we will go there and get in deep trouble that not even the "magic" can get us out of!"

"Girl, chilllll," Kris said exasperatedly, "stop being so paranoid; nothing's gonna happen for heaven's sake! You have to trust Nathan!"

"Why should I trust someone who's definitely gonna ditch us if we get caught?"

Kris didn't answer.

At 10:15 A.M. a grinchy me, a jolly Kris, an excited Selene, and an ecstatic Nathan went to carry out our "plaza chores" at the same time. We had to go extra early because we had to walk an awfully long way to get near where Kris and I used to live. After fifteen minutes of running, things began to look familiar. I saw the railway station and the buildings Kris and I often hid behind. I even spotted the exact spot on the streets where Kris and I once sat. We both looked at it for a few seconds before continuing behind Nathan and Selene.

When we arrived Downtown, we could see a sign reading 'Holiday Festival.' All around the downtown area there were bobbing for apples areas, huge piles of yellow, orange, and red leaves, and the occasional pumpkin and scarecrow. There were artificial rectangular hay bales, and I remembered taking a selfie with Kris on one once.

I smiled as I remembered everything.

"Here we are!" Nathan shouted as we approached a large crowd of people. "The parade! There are ropes so you shouldn't cross them. Also, we should split into pairs because Poppy Parrot wouldn't give four kids four ribs in the same spot. So, me and Selene, and Ari and Kris."

"How are we gonna find each other afterwards, then?" Kris asked. "We'll meet by the scarecrow," Nathan said pointing, "and don't get friendly with people!"

"I can promise you that!" I called before they disappeared into the crowd. I took Kris's hand and we squeezed in near to the brown rope we weren't allowed to cross, next to a woman talking to her friends.

The woman turned to look at us, and then back to her friends. "I'm telling you man," she whispered. "Kids nowadays are nothin' but skin and bones."

A man with a glittery red hat came out and stood in the street where all the floats were supposed to pass by. "Hello, everybody!" he shouted enthusiastically, "Hello! Thank you all for coming, we're eternally grateful! I know it's a couple of minutes after 11:00…" He checked his watch. "But there were some difficulties with some of…the parade…participants…but don't worry that will soon be resolved!" The man walked away.

"I need to use the bathroom," I said, slipping out of the crowd away from Kris.

"Ariiii!" Kris called, "we're supposed to be staying together! Don't…" I had walked away from the crowd before I could hear anything else.

I asked a woman standing in the middle of nowhere where the bathroom was. She pointed to three portable toilets and then she asked: "What went so wrong in your life that you are standing in front of me like this?"

I was thinking of walking away, but instead answered: "Everything." Then I jogged away from her but instead of heading to the toilets, I hung around a tiny shack where loud noises were coming from. I heard two angry voices.

Voice Number One: "John, I am not wearing this! It feels too stuffed, and how will I know when to get all of this?"

Voice Number Two: "When the time is right, now go on! We're already delaying people. Put on your head and go on out there as the happy chirpy birdie you are." I heard a little shuffling, then voice number one shouting: "UGH! This feels like little stones are smashing the side of my head!"

Voice Number Two: "Just relax…this way you can give more people in the audience treats. Just ribs won't cut it."

There was even more shuffling.

Voice Number One: "Oh, goodness, what if I get severely hurt by wearing this stupid thing?"

Voice Number Two: "In the contract, it says we will pay all medical bills. Now let's get this part on straight…"

Then there was a long silence. Right before I decided to go back to the portable toilet and wait for the parade to start, the voices started all over again.

Voice Number One: "Alrighty, I will only be able to make it for a few minutes with this on. Well, John, how do I look? Sweet as back in the day?"

There was a whistle and the tiniest chuckle. "Poppy Parrot surely doesn't look so sweet anymore...Anyway, go on…"

I swung open a portable toilet's door and swung myself inside. I heard a door creak open and footsteps on the gravel. When I was certain Poppy Parrot and his assistant were gone, I left the portable toilet and began walking towards the crowd of people once again.

I felt somebody grab my hand and turn to see if that was Kris. "Ari, where have you been?" she cried. "The parade is about to start, c'mon!" We ran towards the parade.

I fidgeted as band music began playing. Not many people were interested in us once everything started. There were trumpets and drums and people playing triangles. There were several floats, most of them being fall-related. On all the floats there were either ladies dancing or people in costumes waving. I saw Selene's favorite person in the parade, the lady with an M&M on her head waving at all of us.

It could've been anybody in the crowd, but I think I heard Selene squeal happily as she waved. I honestly was having such a great time.

The same man with the glittery red hat came running back onto the parade route. "You know him as a rib-giving, loving guy," he announced. "You know him as a cheery orange and red parrot; who on *Earth* are we talking about now?" "POPPY PARROT!" the audience chorused.

"You got it right!" the man shouted, "Here he comes now!" He ran off and we looked down the road. I didn't see Poppy Parrot until he was almost right in front of us.

I literally hollered when I saw him.

Calling him 'not-so-sweet' was an understatement.

Poppy Parrot wasn't as I had pictured him. He was just a tall guy with a detailed costume…and a Mexican accent maybe? Okay, fine, well, he was the most terrifying thing I had ever seen in my life. First of all, he looked all beat up as if some tough guys had walked up to him and given him a few bruises. He was literally *black* in some areas, and extremely dusty. Secondly, about *half* of his orange feathers were either ripped in half or torn off. Thirdly, his eyes seemed to be staring into my soul and I didn't see any black pupils. The part that had been rubbed off was replaced by a black marker.

Before I could run, the *fourth* bad thing about Poppy Parrot came rushing by. About ten little kids around four years of age came screaming into the parade, hopping around Poppy Parrot shrieking some sort of song in an off-key tone: "He's our parrot! The Poppy Parrot! He gives us ribs to eat!" Okay, fine, the kids were downright adorable. Well, maybe they were adorable. All the kids were wearing parrot heads and the rest of their body was in the usual boy/girl attire of skirts and jeans.

So, basically, there was a dead-looking parrot and ten kids with parrot heads but no parrot bodies. Kris took my hand in hers. I could just picture Nathan clapping along, grinning at the stupidity. It would take a lot of love to like this thing.

The kids scurried off eventually back to their parents, almost knocking people over. "Hi, there!" Poppy Parrot cried, sounding almost strained, "how's everybody doing?" He almost screamed that last part.

Everybody cheered.

Poppy Parrot put his hands on his huge head. "Oh, my goodness," he murmured softly, "John! When am I supposed to get this thing off? I can't take it any longer! Can't I just give it to the children?"

There was no reply.

"John!" Poppy Parrot screamed, now on his knees. I chewed my lip, laughing. I liked to see him suffer. This parade was gonna be an epic failure. Then, one of the most astonishing things happened that made me stop cackling.

Poppy Parrot exploded.

CHAPTER 14

The Letter

Everybody screamed. I mean, it wasn't all bad that Poppy Parrot had exploded. He wasn't dead. He was flat on the ground, but I didn't think he was dead. I hoped somebody knew CPR because when I tried to learn it didn't go so well...

Poppy Parrot had exploded with chocolates. Chocolates of all varieties and sizes with all sorts of different wrappings. Poppy Parrot shouted and squirmed on the ground. His parrot head had come off. He was just a man with black hair now.

The brown rope suddenly vibrated and before anyone could blink, Nathan was helping Poppy Parrot up. And then Selene hopped over and began helping as well.

I felt Ari wriggling her hand away from mine and slipping under the brown rope as well.

"Ariiii!" I said, "where are you going?"

"I'm gonna help him so that I can get a rib!" Ari whispered loudly. I followed her and helped Poppy Parrot up. By this time, kids were stealing the idea of sucking up and began approaching, crowding around. "I was the one who helped you up," a boy lied. "No, I was!" a girl about seven screamed.

"No, you weren't, we were!" I said to the little girl, now screaming more lies. Somebody tripped over the plate of ribs that was on the ground and the ribs plummeted off it and onto the road. Most of the kids left but me, Ari, Selene, and Nathan grabbed one each from off the road along with two other boys there.

I kept nibbling as we went back into the crowd; a lady was still watching us. Finally, she nudged me and asked: "Would your parents really approve of you eating off the ground like that?"

I didn't know what to say to her. I knew it was rude, but I shrugged. The woman scoffed. "Where are your parents anyway?" she murmured softly, looking around.

Ari and I exchanged glances.

"You shouldn't be left alone," the woman continued, "why are they just leaving you here? Have they run off to get food or something?"

I didn't respond.

"It's rude not to reply when an adult is speaking to you!"

This was usual. There were some overly concerned people who wanted to know why we weren't snuggled up to our mom or dad or something. But I was frozen.

"Um," I said, searching for one of our usual lies, "they got stuck somewhere…they'll be here soon." I put my hand over my eyes and scanned the food stands, pumpkins, scarecrows, and grass as if I were searching for them. "In fact, I think they're right over there." I pointed to some random people ordering some hotdogs at a stand.

"Yeah," Ari chimed in.

"I bet your parents don't want you to look like cockroaches covered in dirt," the woman joked savagely.

"They might give us some good clothes later," I explained, "they want some time without stressing about the kids." Ari nodded and we both smiled sweetly.

"Yeah, uh-huh…" the woman said, "How about I pop up to your parents and ask them why they aren't protecting you from strangers?" She sounded like she believed us and was plain mad at our so-called "parents."

She stomped away and Ari and I automatically searched the crowd for Nathan and Selene. We practically had to drag them away from the parade, which was still in full swing.

"Well, wasn't that amazing?" Selene asked as we went back Downtown. "Yeah," Nathan stated, "it just keeps getting better every year."

We continued strolling, ducking behind the buildings, and walking alongside the disgusting train station. "Why did you lie about your parents?" Selene inquired after a long silence.

"Because it's what we do," Ari replied quickly.

"Sure, but it went wrong, didn't it?" Nathan observed.

"Shut up, Nate," I muttered.

"I just don't get it," Ari noted, kicking a pebble, "lying has gotten us out of most of our problems, and now it just got us into one."

"Maybe you guys should tell the truth," Nathan suggested. "I mean, if you had done it from the start, you guys would've been in a foster home or a REAL orphanage or whatever."

"Oh yippee," Ari cheered sarcastically, then stopped. "Maybe it would have been better…but I don't know."

"I feel like it would be." Ari looked at me. "I mean, it would have spared us the fire…we wouldn't be here. It's like it's almost our fault for making bad decisions; why couldn't we just have been more responsible and…"

"When did this conversation get so dark?" Nathan interrupted, "I mean at first we're talking about the parade and now about fires, responsibility and decisions!"

"We could have been more responsible," I insisted.

"Sis, The Diamond Square *is* responsibility," Ari urged, raising her head up. But a part of me is thinking differently.

Every Thursday we had to clean the dormitory because Mrs. Sesmore came in and checked it. We had finished all our cleaning, dusting, sweeping, and scrubbing and were playing Pokeno, a card game.

Mrs. Sesmore pushed open the door, looking a bit confused. Ari and Nathan began packing the Pokeno away. Mrs. Sesmore stepped in, forced a smile, looked around and said: "Uh, hello…" She looked at me. "Kristina…you have…a letter…you can read it in the library…" Then she slammed the door before inspecting anything. Selene ran back out to get her. I grabbed the door before it swung closed, looked at Nathan and Ari, who both shrugged and stepped out of the room.

I wandered around a little bit before I saw a room with loads of bookcases and books. Dad would have loved this place. There was a small desk and on top of it was a feather and a tiny black box. There was an envelope that read:

DREXEL HALL
RETURNING ADDRESS: #256 OLDERT SWENUE STREET
CLEVELAND, OHIO

      KRISTINA COOPER
      WENSLEY ALFORD STREET
      CLEVELAND, OHIO
        UNITED STATES OF AMERICA

I ripped open the envelope and read the letter tucked inside.

DEAR KRISTINA,

It's me, Drexel, from school. Well, I didn't expect you and your sister to come back to school right away, but I got worried after a few days soo…I just asked teachers. They said they hadn't seen you guys either, but one of them had your guardian's number. That Axel guy? We called him but he wouldn't answer. So, the teacher gave me a photo of both of you guys and I copied it and posted MISSING signs of you guys.

Turns out a lot of people got involved and I was biking farther in town to get more and more posters out when this girl in a fancy black car took one look at it and said that you're at this Diamond Square place. She gave me the address and told me I can write letters, so…here I am, I guess.

The girl must've been Emily. Who else at The Diamond Square besides Emily would have some fancy black car…even though I've never seen it…but still…….

I don't know if you can write back because I have no idea how you guys wound up in The Diamond Square. Is it like an orphanage? Do you like it there? Are there diamonds?

I wish.

Well, if there are, you're super lucky and super lucky to skip out on all these stupid quizzes…
From, Drexel.

That's it. *How can I write back to him?* I thought. I'm not surprised Cindy wasn't in this letter. I put the letter back in the envelope and left the library. As I expected, Mrs. Sesmore was in the main room at her little desk where she checked people in.

"Um, excuse me." I cleared my throat.

Mrs. Sesmore looked up from her desk.

"How can I write back to Drexel?" I inquired.

"Who's Drexel?"

"The person who wrote me," I explained impatiently. "Am I allowed to write him back?"

Mrs. Sesmore sighed. "I'm sure the ink in the library has run out," she announced. "Shouldn't you be doing your chores anyway?" she added.

"Is there any way I can *fill* the ink bottle and make that one of my chores?" I questioned. Mrs. Sesmore tapped her pen against her chin, avoiding eye contact with me. Somebody pushed open the big door to get outside. "There's a book in the library about making homemade ink," Mrs. Sesmore said, "it's underneath the ink stand."

I ran back to the library before Mrs. Sesmore could stop me. I opened the door and looked under the inkstand. Tada! A dusty brown book was lying peacefully underneath it. I opened it and looked at the chapters. In worn out letters it stated:

Chapter 9: Making Ink–Page 243.

I flipped the pages and read the instructions for making ink.

Black food coloring

One egg

Add honey.

Across the page there were words written by other servants. Things like:

Do not try this foolishness. Had to make my own PINK ink. If you don't like the color pink, you suck.

Lara S.

Lara, please stop your foolishness before we get in trouble.

Peter Simpson

Stop writing in the book, guys!"

I grabbed a few things from the kitchen to make the ink. I found a book of lined paper and began writing:

To Drexel,

Hey!!! :) I just saw your letter· You went through a whole lot just to find us· I guess the 'Missing' Posters are alright...I don't think The Diamond Square is an orphanage because there are grown-ups here and older teens· Boy, I don't like a THING about this place and... diamonds...· I don't think there are any diamonds...but I could look for some!

From, Kristina (from school)

I had run out of things to say or questions to answer. Then I looked at the ink ingredients and all of the things people had written in the book. I decided to make my name known too. I picked up the feather pen and began writing my own words right next to Lara's declaration where she could see it.

Lara the recipe isn't even that hard· Read it over, friend·

Kristina was here!!! :>

I put the face to taunt her. I put the feather pen down and looked at it for a few moments. Mrs. Sesmore walked in and told me that I needed to stop messing around and do my tasks. I opened a drawer, found stacked envelopes, and put my letter in one. I wet the envelope with a little tap water.

I put The Diamond Square's address and my full name on it. If I had any plaza chores, I'd have to go all the way to the post office and mail my letter to Drexel. I can't even believe that he remembered me after all this time.

I told Mrs. Sesmore I was going to dust the bookshelves in the library and even though she commented that she hardly considered that a task, she let me do it anyway. Instead of doing that, I used my feather pen and wrote stuff in all sorts of books. I sat down in the old, dusty, worn-out, fluffy easy chair and began writing. Whenever somebody else walked in, I grabbed the big duster that was right next to me and pretended to be dusting the dirt off the book, and then continued writing once they had left. Lara was in every book. She must never have done her tasks if she had time to write all of this.

After a while, my stomach growled. I put down the book I was writing in, grabbed the letter I had written and snuck out of the library and down the hall into the main room. A man was standing in the doorway and Mrs. Sesmore was talking to him. I walked over to them and waited for them to pause.

"Yes?" Mrs. Sesmore turned to me.

"Um," I began, "I didn't have breakfast today so I'm hungry. So can I go and…"

"You are not permitted to go there," Mrs. Sesmore declared firmly, hands on her hips.

"But…"   "

 "Buts are not permitted in The Diamond Square," Mrs. Sesmore interrupted, "end of conversation."

I rolled my eyes and waited for Mrs. Sesmore to continue talking to the man. It would take more than a lecture to stop Kristina Cooper.

I went into the hallway a little like I was sauntering back into the library, but I wasn't about to do that.

"So, what's the problem?" the man asked as I cautiously crawled to the cafeteria. "A rotten child broke off a piece of the wall," Mrs. Sesmore replied, and then there was a sort of hitting, banging noise, wherever that came from.

Trying to mind my own business, I got a spoon out of the sink, and walked over to the metal bowls with almost no food inside of them. By now, the girls were staring at me. I leaned into a metal bowl and spooned out something that was lumpy and vaguely beige-colored. I spooned it into my mouth. It tasted like nothing at all.

One of the girls with a dirty blonde bob cleared her throat. "We were actually planning on saving that for later," she muttered, as I continued to have my fill.

I popped my head back out of the metal bowl and grinned at them. I don't know why, honestly. Then I dived back in, leaning forward until I completely fell inside of the metal tub of food! I scrambled around anxiously until the metal bowl fell off the counter and onto the floor and the tub made the *biggest, most enormous* clang.

Uh-oh.

Mrs. Sesmore came running in with the same man who was with her in the hallway. He had a blueprint in his arms.

"What is going on?" Mrs. Sesmore shrieked, "what is…" Mrs. Sesmore spotted me on the floor completely covered with beige whatever-it-was. She blinked, her mouth still hanging open. "How did you get in there…?" she stammered, "oh…young lady you are in so much…"

"But it's not my fault!" I interrupted, searching for more lies, "the girl there pushed me in!" I pointed to the girl with the bob and her friend. Her friend shook her head and clutched the girl with the bob's hand.

Mrs. Sesmore turned to the girls. "What are your names, again?" she asked them.

"My name is Tristie," she muttered in a shaky voice, "and this…," she pointed to the other girl- "th…this is Jamie." Jamie had pecan-colored hair that almost covered her eyes but not in a *scary* way. More like in a *scary* kind of way because Jamie's eyes were round and fearful, obviously waiting for the worst.

"Did you witness what happened?" Mrs. Sesmore snapped at Jamie. Jamie's eyes went wide, and she hid behind Tristie. She looked like she was about eight years old.

"She did not see anything," Tristie said.

Mrs. Sesmore moved right behind the counter so Jamie would have to face her. Jamie shivered. "Now, don't act stupid." Jamie gulped and covered her hands with her face and whispered something ever so quietly.

"Louder, child!" Mrs. Sesmore demanded.

"Please don't hurt Tristie," she squeaked in a whispery tone, "please don't hurt her." Jamie looked at Tristie, whose mouth was wide open in shock.

"And why not?"

"Because she didn't do anything wrong!" Jamie stomped her foot. And then immediately withdrew it (too late). She whimpered with fear, crouched on the floor and began sobbing. She was so cute and adorable. I wanted to reach down and give her a hug.

But I was still sitting up on the floor, looking like a melting tanned snowman with no buttons for eyes or a carrot nose. Tristie was frozen, and then stuttered: "I literally thought you couldn't talk…" Jamie shrugged.

Mrs. Sesmore sent the girls to their dorms and told them not to return at lunch or dinner. They both ran away crying. I felt kind of guilty. But, hey, Mrs. Sesmore believed *me* over them!

I went outside and walked all the way to the spring. I put my clothes in for a few seconds to clean them off and then put them on the grass beside the spring to get dried by the strong wind. When I was done, I hopped into my damp clothes and went back inside The Diamond Square.

Mrs. Sesmore was in the doorway of the screen door. "You took forever in there," she commented, "how about you stop dusting the library and go ahead with all of your other chores?" It was a demand…not a suggestion.

I begrudgingly began doing my actual chores. None of them was at the plaza though, so I couldn't mail my letter.

I went outside and grabbed a rake. I helped the other two kids who were raking leaves put them into a huge pile. The best part about it was that the kids were younger and smaller than I was, so I was able to look out for them and correct them, just like a responsible and caring big sister would.

CHAPTER 15

Renovation

"WHAT HAVE YOU DONE, CHILD?" Mrs. Sesmore screamed at me. We both stared at the huge chunk of gray concrete that was right in front of the main door. The door in the front of The Diamond Square, the one Emily and Mistress Smith would enter from. I had no idea how I had managed to accomplish this. I had my back against a wall, foot leaning on it too, and then a piece of wall literally fell off. It got to snag my bare, vulnerable foot too, and now there was a scar.

"Do you know how bad this would look to so many people?" Mrs. Sesmore inquired. "Do you even know how old this brick is?" I shook my head. "It's one hundred and fifty-six years old," Mrs. Sesmore continued, "one hundred and fifty-six years old!"

"Maybe that's why it broke," I told her. Mrs. Sesmore hurried away, obviously going to tell Mr. Waite. Before she left, she ordered me to go the Punishment Room.

Fifteen minutes of boredom later, Mrs. Sesmore came in, carrying blue paper under her arm. "I had to call one of my old classmates to come over," she stated, puffing. "He recommends we get a new wall and have a complete *renovation*! And you know something? All because you broke a piece of wall!" She stared at the blue paper (which turned out to be a blueprint) and sighed. "Showers...? Room with chairs for announcements...?" she muttered, "how is this ever going to work?"

"Can I leave now?" I asked.

"Change of plans, you're going to be doing your chores instead," Mrs. Sesmore replied. She sighed. I leaped out of my chair, checked my list, but was extremely confused about what my next task was.

Plant berry bush (your choice... just don't make it poison)

"I'm planting a berry bush?" I asked.

"Of course, you are!"

"But a berry bush? Why a berry bush?"

"Because we want you to plant a berry bush!" Mrs. Sesmore slammed the blueprint on her desk in frustration. I really didn't want to bother Mrs. Sesmore again, but I didn't know where to find any berry bush *seeds*. After that reaction, however, I had an inkling of an idea that the number of questions I was allowed was up.

I looked down, fumbling with my hands. Somebody knocked on the door. "Come in!" Mrs. Sesmore called. The door creaked as Mr. Waite stepped into the room.

Uh-oh.

Mrs. Sesmore rolled up the blueprint and looked at him. "Well," she remarked, "didn't think you'd stop by." Mrs. Sesmore took the rolled-up blueprint and tapped it on her desk. I squirmed and tried to figure out a way to get out of this mess quickly.

"Ah, hello," Mr. Waite remarked, "almost didn't see you there." He turned to Mrs. Sesmore. "Did you bring these people over here? What are they *doing?*"

"Renovating," Mrs. Sesmore answered briefly, "they think it would be best to give the "old' jack in the box" a new look. A new style."

Mr. Waite shook his head. "I have a bad feeling about this new look," he muttered after a while, then turned to me. "Do you know how much you are costing us?" he demanded sharply. "Good grief! Children!"

He walked out of the room, talking quietly to himself, probably thinking about renovation costs and all that. "Why are you still here?" Mrs. Sesmore asked once Mr. Waite was gone. "How am I going to plant the berry bush if I don't have any seeds?" I queried.

Mrs. Sesmore looked like she was about to say something, but then stopped and thought, staring into space. It was obvious she hadn't thought this whole thing through. I fumbled with my hands for a bit longer. Suddenly, Mrs. Sesmore's head snapped up. "I know!" she announced, "you can go to the plaza and purchase berry bush seeds." She handed me five dollars. I took it. Mrs. Sesmore continued and said that on the right side of the plaza there was a small store called 'Bushy's Supplements.' She told me that I could find seeds there.

"Don't take too long!" shouted Mrs. Sesmore as I stepped out of the door, "and don't get lost, for goodness' sakes!" There was a loud noise as I closed the door. I walked down the hallway and was surprised to see men at the entry of our doorway, with dusty clothes and heavy equipment. There were also huge, strange vehicles in the front of The Diamond Square. These people weren't kidding when they said there was going to be an extensive renovation here.

I stared at them for a moment and then walked to the screen door, snapped it open and then closed it shut. It was a windy day, and goosebumps began to form on my arms. I saw Kris in The Diamond Square yard, raking the yellow, orange and red leaves into piles.

She spotted me and waved. I jogged up to her and grinned a huge smile. "What?"

I showed her the five-dollar bill. "This."

Kris stared at it for a while. "Wait," she demanded, "wait, wait, wait, did you steal that?"

"No!" I shook my head. "Mrs. Sesmore told me to go to the plaza and find some store to buy berry bush seeds."

Kris raised an eyebrow. "What would that woman do with berry bush seeds?"

"I know, right?"

Kris dug into her muddy, dirty (and now red, orange, and yellow leaf-covered) pockets, pulled out a white envelope with smudges on it and handed it to me. "Since you're going to the plaza can you stop and post this for me?"

"What is it?" I took it and examined it from all angles. "It's a letter I wrote to Drexel," Kris explained, "that's why Mrs. Sesmore called me out earlier today."

"Oh." I put it in my almost-ready-to-fall-off-pocket that was unravelling quickly. "He wrote to you?"

"Mhmm. He did."

"I thought everybody forgot about us," I noted bitterly, getting ready to leave.

"Well, he didn't," Kris answered. "He even tried to call Axel…but he didn't answer. And then he put MISSING signs of us all over town…and then some girl, I think it was Emily, told him where we were, and our address and he sent me this letter."

I blinked and shook my head. Then I went toward the plaza and headed for Bushy's Supplement Store.

Bushy's was a tiny, tiny store and it took me 10 minutes to find it. I opened the glass door's red handle and a bell jingled as I came in. There were rows of shelves that were silver and shining under the beams of sunlight. The shelves were well stocked with cookies, room temperature water, crackers, snacks, bread and seeds. A few broken toys were piled in an old kid's treasure chest which was partly hidden in a corner.

There were three people in the shop-- a man with a stubby graying beard, a heavy guy sitting in a swivel chair behind a cash register and me. There were only four shelves, so finding the seeds would be easy.

I looked at each of the four shelves twice, but I couldn't find any seeds. "You need help?" the heavy guy grunted. I nodded. "What ya need help with?" he grumbled. "Um," I responded, "do you have any seeds?"

"Yep," the heavy guy muttered, "you want daises, daffodils or what?"

"Berry bush seeds," I answered. The heavy guy got up and went outside. The bell rang. I blinked, stifling a scoff, or maybe a laugh, maybe a little bit of both. I was literally talking to him, and he just walked out of the door?

I concluded that he would just walk back in. The rare times when this happens in movies or TV shows or whatever, they always come right back. The shoe man leaves, the characters get sad, the shoe man comes back with the greatest shoes of your entire life! The policeman leaves, the people give up all hope, and then the policeman comes back with the guilty man!

I paced around the store, played with the broken toys, snuck a few goodies into my will-probably-be-gone-by-next-month pockets for me, Kris, Selene, and Nathan to snack on later. Half an hour passed, and the heavy guy had still not returned.

He had abandoned me.

I wandered around and checked the shelves once again. In fact, I picked up every item, inspected it, looked behind it, looked at the item on the left or right of it, then the item above and below it.

The other customer had left a long time ago, just a couple of minutes after the heavy guy had left, in fact. My stomach had been growling for the past hour, and I was hungry. I was about to shoplift my behind out of the store when I tripped over something that felt like branches.

WOOMPH. I cascaded onto the floor, my arms and legs flailing in the air. I slowly picked myself up and looked behind me. There was a basket on the floor, and something was spilling out of it. I reached inside and pulled out a card that read:

AL'S

DELICIOUS PUMPKIN SEEDS

$4.99 (including tax)

I reached into the basket again and pulled out a packet of raspberry seeds. The thing about these pumpkin and raspberry seeds was that they looked smushed and disgusting. I pulled out five more packets until I found a blueberry one.

AL'S
SCRUMPTIOUS BLUEBERRY SEEDS
2.99 (including tax)

I grabbed the blueberry seed packet, slapped down three dollars on the counter and began walking out of the door. As I left, the overhead bell jangled loudly.

I had almost forgotten to post Kristina's letter, but I remembered when the pointy white paper poked out of my thin pockets. I had to get instructions from a nearby post office worker. He was a tough cookie. He wouldn't tell me where the blue and white post office was until I gave him seventy-five cents.

I walked inside and tried to mail the letter as fast as I could. Sadly, that wasn't possible because the lady was more concerned with the fact that my name was Ari, while the letter said the writer was Kristina. It took me ten whole minutes to prove to her I wasn't doing a scam of any sort. She even *read* the whole letter!!! Is that even legal?

Fifty minutes later than I wanted to leave, I headed back from the plaza to The Diamond Square. I almost forgot about the bridge, because the only times I had been here was just to do unreasonable errands. I stopped to study the bridge and smiled when the sun twinkled against it. I didn't go back there because it wasn't right or necessary. Besides, I needed every ounce of sleep I could get.

The sounds of a chainsaw echoed as I walked toward The Diamond Square. As I approached the garden where Kris and the two kids were raking leaves, they were gone and a group of men pointing and laughing replaced them. I quickly opened the screen door and went inside. The Diamond Square was warm and comforting. No servants were rushing around to get their chores done. Men and women were wearing yellow hats and blue paper was flying everywhere. I ran over to the Punishment Room, and even Mrs. Sesmore wasn't there. Somebody tapped me on the back.

"Hello, where are you supposed to be?" It was a man with a yellow helmet and a rolled-up blueprint. "Um," I began, looking at the floor, "I got these for Mrs. Sesmore." I held up the blueberry seeds to him. The man looked at them for a millisecond, apparently automatically bored. "I would plant them myself," he noted apologetically, "but I ain't got no business in 'em. You are supposed to be in your rooms. Ain't supposed to be here."

He turned and jogged away, shouting at somebody that they weren't doing something right. I went to the dormitory and found Nathan, Selene, and Kris sitting on their beds. They all looked at me.

"Good, you're here." Selene fixed herself on her bed. "Now I can finally say what I've overheard."

"What have you overheard?" I asked, walking over to my bed, and sitting up on it.

"So," Selene whispered, causing us to all lean in, "I think the reason they're doing the renovation is because I heard Mrs. Sesmore and Mr. Waite are thinking of advertising."

"Advertising?" Nathan asked.

"Yeah," Selene insisted, "like going around saying that you can stay here at The Diamond Square, no money, no fees. Just you have to behave or else."

"I'd ask 'or else what?'" Kris murmured, staring at the ceiling. "They'd probably lie," I told her. "Maybe say something pathetic to trap you or whatever."

Everybody was silent.

"Alright." Nathan hopped onto the floor and began digging under his bed. That's where we kept all our games. It was the only place to keep them. He pulled out Monopoly and grinned.

Monopoly was his favorite game.

We were buying properties, throwing the dice, and moving our characters when we heard shuffling and loud voices right in front of our door. At first, we ignored the noises because they were next door. But now all the clanking seemed to be near to us.

There was a knock on the door. Kris got up to answer it. To our surprise, there were five men and two ladies. They were all pitching in to carry two beds. Selene frowned and began putting away the game. Nathan protested (because he was winning) but the people came in with two beds wrapped in plastic. Kris was stepping aside, and we needed to clear up.

Four of them rested the beds down carefully in the middle of the room while three of them squished our beds closer together. Then they formed a group to make one extra bed. So now mine and Kristina's bed had been pushed together even more so that there could now be three in our row instead of just two. It was the same for Nathan and Selene.

We didn't say anything, just backed up against the wall that held the one window in our tiny space. They had just intruded on us.

"Uh," Nathan who was the first one with the nerve to speak, asked, "what are you doing?"

"We were ordered to put extra beds in here," a man answered, taking the plastic covering off the bed, "so that each dormitory will have exactly six beds each. They're hoping some new people will be arriving soon, I believe."

Selene gave us a 'see, I was right!' face and nodded. A worker kicked the dusty wooden planks on the floor in disgust. "A place like this needs detailed tile," she commented, picking at some hard stuff in between the floorboards, "but tile needs to be swept and mopped thoroughly, though." The lady kicked the floor again and shook her head.

When they had removed the plastic covering, they left, saying that they would be coming back later because each dorm needed to have two extra beds. Each dorm would also need new flooring.

Well, that's what the lady said.

CHAPTER 16

Evicted!

A minute after all the guys left, a speaker in our room announced: "PLEASE COME TO THE MAIN ROOM FOR AN IMPORTANT ANNOUNCEMENT." Then it went silent. All of us in the room walked out in single file. I lost everyone in the mob of people running down the stairs.

It was loud and noisy in the main room with all the heavy equipment rumbling outside. Mr. Waite looked around and declared: "A friend of ours suggested a renovation of the entire Diamond Square. So, of course, we are beginning to do that. In the meantime, you might have to find another place to stay. That's not written in stone, but……. Mr. Waite's voice trailed off. "Also, we have even thought of hiring more maids to help around here. They're only "auditioning." We're going to see their level of… "maid intelligence." Due to the renovation, maid hiring and a crowd of kid shelters begging to give us bunches of children, we have developed a problem. We seem to be just hovering above the rim of bankruptcy…"

Despite the chainsaw ripping through wood nearby, everything seemed to have gone silent.

"…and so, as a result, we may have to cut some people from The Diamond Square."

"Jesus keep the wheel," I prayed silently.

The woman with the chainsaw kept on sawing the wood in half, obviously enjoying the task.

"We realized," Mr. Waite continued, "that it would be much better to do…this plan. People who are eighteen years and older will be…sort of…shoved away from The Diamond Square. They need most of the food and cause most of our problems. Adults have to start thinking and start moving because in a few days they had better have everything in place to go ahead and move on."

Terrified gasps went around.

"Now," Mr. Waite stated, "as I said, eighteen and older can please start evacuating The Diamond Square." There were a few cries and some grumbling. Suddenly, a familiar red-headed boy emerged from the crowd, and I realized it was the same teen who had picked on me earlier.

"But that's not *fair*," he whined, "I'll have to be out and about in *five months*. It's not fair. You don't own us!" He stomped his foot. Mrs. Sesmore went into her desk, dug for an awfully long time, and took out a sheet of paper. Shoving it in his face she said smartly: "Norman, in this contract, you are banished when we banish you. Especially little troublemakers."

I shuddered.

"I'm not a troublemaker!" he shouted, snatching the contract, and pointing wildly to it, "in this here contract, it also says you will take care of me! This is not taking care of me!"

Mrs. Sesmore pointed to a sentence at the bottom of the contract that read: "RULES MAY VARY." Norman stared at it and his face went tomato red. He grabbed the contract and ripped it up, his face still red.

"NOBODY'S GOING TO HIRE ME!" he shouted, pointing a shaking finger at Mrs. Sesmore.

"Yep," she answered, perfectly calm, "nobody will with that horrible temper." Norman threw up his hands and stomped back into the crowd, covering his face.

One third of me was like: *Serves you right, trying to pin my wrong on me and picking on me.'* And the other part: 'Goodness, nobody IS gonna hire him with a temper like that.' and the last: *'I hope he finds a job.'*

"You are dismissed," Mr. Waite finished it all. "Finish your tasks that are outside, please." People were 'boo-ing' and 'that's not fair!.' I was about to go outside to start raking some more leaves when I felt a tug on my shoulder. I spun around and saw Nathan and Selene.

"We have to find a place to stay," he proposed. I smacked his hand off my shoulder. Annoyed, I complained: "Why don't you and Selene find a place?"

"Because WE…" He gestured to himself and Selene. "…Need to keep an eye on YOU!" He now pointed at me and my sister who, it seemed, had magically appeared.

"Or we're just friends!" Selene suggested, grinning, and jumping up and down. Nathan looked at her, and then said: "Noo! Now, come on, let's find someplace."

For a bit we walked around the main room, saw people hugging and crying, people throwing tantrums and people attempting to knock out Mr. Waite's eyeballs. Yep, that seemed to be the new normal here at The Diamond Square.

Selene stopped in front of the huge, dusty fireplace. "How about here?" she asked. I shook my head. "Nah," I protested, "we would die of coughing and hacking."

It took us about an hour, but we found a spot in the library. It may not have had board games, but it did have lots of books. It also had a comfy chair that we were going to take turns sleeping in.

"Okay," Nathan announced, "now that we've decided on where we're going to stay, I guess now we get to do our outdoor chores.

I smiled, eager to find the little kids again. I started out of the door and down the stairs. I whipped open the screen door, took a few steps and sat down on the grassy ground, waiting for the two kids to come.

They didn't come the way I had expected.

They each ran in from opposite sides of The Diamond Square and collapsed on my lap, giggling. Okaaay, then. Ari was planting her seeds in a moist dirt patch nearby and I kept daydreaming about going home to our comfortable apartment that we shared with Aunt Maybelle. Wait…

The dust in here was killing me, but I had to get this done. I clutched the feather pen, dipped it in my homemade black ink (which was half-way full) and began writing.

Hi, Aunt Maybelle! It's me, Kristina. After the fire we were kidnapped by a mean man who dumped us on the streets. We ended up in an orphanage, where they never gave us enough food and we worked like slaves. You will be Super Auntie if you come and rescue us.
Love Kristina

P.S. Remember when you were going to some ball, and somebody was babysitting me, Ari and Kasie? And I said the dress you were wearing looked good, but just didn't look good on you? I didn't mean that. I was lying to you. That dress looked amazing on you! :>

I read it over, proud of my work, stuffed it in my almost-gone pocket, smiled, and snuck back outside to the plaza to mail my creation. As I was searching, I couldn't help thinking that hey, this was a surprisingly good plan. Aunt Maybelle couldn't just *leave* us here. She would take us back home. Right? Right…?

Right…

Why was I doubting my own aunt? Of course, she would take us home…. Then it hit me like a ton of bricks. I have no idea where my aunt is.

I told Ari my plan that evening, while we were pacing outside, waiting for somebody to come out and tell us that we would be able to stay here. We were sitting on the ground near a busy anthill, plucking at grass.

"Soo, girl, what do you think?" I asked Ari, watching the sun slowly go down.

"About what?"

"About my plan."

"Oh. Yeah, I think it's workable! It's not like Aunt Maybelle can say no."

"Yeah," I shifted myself up, feeling proud, "because family always has each other's back."

We were waiting for dinner…if we were going to have dinner. The sun was setting and there were still chainsaws running. I had no idea why the workers were still here, but they were getting a little annoying. They didn't seem to care much that we were still moving about.

All day we had been dilly-dallying outside, finishing our outdoor chores, and all the while Ari and I were begging God that somehow our letter would get to Aunt Maybelle, and she would come to take us home. The sun was getting lower and lower, and the sky was deep orange on one side but purple and pink on the other.

I had never seen a sunset like this, and boy, was it spectacular! A few moments later (or maybe hours, I don't know) Mrs. Sesmore came outside and began yelling that it was dinner time. Everybody stampeded over each other to get in first. I tried to pry a person out of the way to get through the screen door. There was a lot of yelling until we got into the lunchroom.

Mostly women were flying about, arguing, or trying their best to serve. I served myself some red mush and peas and quickly went to my seat.

Boy, did this place get cold easily! Day after day the frost began to gather up a lot more on the windows, and finally…it happened. Ari and I had never minded when we could skip school, wake up our parents to ask them for our gear, and race outside to play. When the blizzard completely covered the entire street, we would run for shelter inside. There were so many memories of what we used to do. So, don't judge, if thirteen-year-old me woke up, and started getting so excited about what was outside the window when I saw…

"SNOW!" I screamed. Everyone's head popped up. The library was dark, but the window was all the proof I needed. My eyes identically sparkled with Ari's as we looked outside at the white flakes floating past the tiny window. Selene clapped her hands and Nathan gave a faint whoop, then flopped back down on the carpet.

The last few days led to a little crescendo, bringing the chilly winds and frost. Snow was coming. Women and just a few men were serving us food now and swarming around the place like annoying bees. Today was actually a big day for almost everyone.

- ☐ A snow day for both Ari and me
- ☐ The decision day for all the maids. Who would be sent home, and who would stay here at the gloomy Diamond Square (a rip-off if you ask me)
- ☐ Today was the last day people eighteen and older could stay. This also meant a busload of new kids would arrive.
- ☐ Starting now, the rules will be stricter. One slip-up and you get caught…you're out.

The morning bell rang, and Nathan groaned. "WELL, LOOK OUTSIDE," the announcer declared, "THE FIRST SNOW DAY OF THE YEAR. LET'S TRY TO GET THE INSIDE CHORES DONE BEFORE THE RENOVATION PEOPLE COME."

In the main room there was a decree. Both the paper and the ink looked old. The paper was torn in some places, but it was still readable.

Good Morning Everybody!

We appear to have a snow day! The same rules apply to EVERY single snow day! First, in the Storage Room there are numerous coats and jackets. Everybody will take one. Some are worse than others so you may want to get there early (the best ones are near the top on your left).

"Same rules since forever," a voice moaned. I kept on staring outside all the windows of The Diamond Square. Yeah, right, like I care if it's snowing. And when you're sick of it and you want it to go away, just throw some good ole' salt on the snow. It would melt away faster than lightning.

Mr. Waite appeared and clapped his hands for attention. "As you can well see," he began, "it is snowing." *Yeah, I'm quite sure we see that Captain Obvious.*

"We only have a week until Christmas," Mr. Waite stated, "so we need to get all the chores done. The busload of children will be arriving at 3:00 PM. *sharp!* Go ahead and start putting on your warm clothes. You'll change them each night. We followed him, pushing, and shoving into a room with a huge closet door. Inside were hundreds of gray, white and yellow jackets.

Like a mob of squeaking, angry rats we charged at the jackets. "I'm not getting the peed-up one this year!" a boy's voice called. "Yeah? We'll see about that!" a strong woman's voice replied. I felt my heart skip a beat in my chest.

I rummaged around and found a comfy enough jacket. It was black and didn't smell *too bad*. At least not somebody-definitely-peed-in-this-stupid-thing bad. I zipped it up and sped outside faster than anybody else.

The atmosphere was freezing, and the ground was mushy like oatmeal. I kicked a little of the snow, feeling carefree. I didn't even care that I had more than a half-dozen chores to do. I also didn't care that Emily was coming on December 25th.

Grinning, I stuck out my tongue and swerved in a circle until the refreshing taste of a newborn snowflake fell onto it. Snow, finally SNOW!

That night was my turn to go on the comfy chair. I lay down on it carefully, breathing peacefully and quietly. I had never, I repeat, NEVER felt so at ease and here I was with my stomach growling, my skin itching, and my knee hurting and scraped from a fall on a rock. I sighed and smiled.

I had never felt so at peace, so at rest. I put my hands under my head and sighed. I closed my eyes and snuggled even closer to the chair and sighed again as if I had too much air in my body and needed to let it all out.

People above 18 had been forced out, and nothing eventful happened then except for lots of crying. And hitting. And one attempt at landing a blow right on Mr. Waite's head. I waved goodbye to all of them, which may sound like I was mocking but I wasn't.

Well, maybe just in Norman's case.

I opened my eyes and sighed, knowing I probably should keep it down because now we were not the only kids here. But I couldn't help sighing! I had been so comfortable for the last forty-five minutes, but I couldn't go to sleep. I could hear tossing and turning from the other side of the library and quiet groans. I pressed against the chair and closed my eyes again, attempting to sleep. I sighed and almost giggled.

"Hey, will you keep it down?" an angry voice called. I stifled another giggle. "Hehe," I whispered, then raised my voice, "Sorry, I'll stop sighing now." I heaved into the chair, laughing mutely. When I calmed down, I finally went to sleep.

CHAPTER 17

Noodle Pie

December 24ᵗʰ

It's nighttime and tomorrow will be Christmas. I guess I'm not as excited as I usually would be because when I wake up, I won't be listening to Christmas music or opening presents from relatives and Kris. It really won't be the same.

Tomorrow, Emily's going to come. All yesterday we found out who our new maids are, and it seems to me like all the nice ones have been fired. And it's ALSO obvious that only the mean ones have enough "maid responsibility" sense.

This can't be my life.

And luckily, it will not be! As soon as Aunt Maybelle responds to our letter, we'll be good to go! We'll live with her FOREVER AND EVER. I can't chance going into an apartment. EVER again! We can save our Moody Moon funds for college instead…Maybe.

"Rudolph, the red-nosed reindeer…"

I blinked even though my eyes were closed. My head was pressed against something hard, like wood. I suddenly realized what was going on. I was on my bed, in our apartment, with Kris right next to me. My head was up against the wood of our bed. Kris probably put the music on with our CD player.

"Had a very shiny nose…"

I smiled, and opened my eyes, which, at the moment were blurry. What a long dream. That was more than long, it was EXCEPTIONALLY long. I sighed, my eyes still blurry, and sighed a sigh of relief. Now it was finally time to start our first day of school, without…

My eyes adjusted. I lifted my head, only to whack it into something hard. I turned my head, expecting to see bed wood and instead I saw a bookshelf holding books. No, no, no, no, no, no, no, NOO! NOOOOOOOOOOOOOOOOOOO! I looked at my palm. I read somewhere that in dreams, the brain can't copy all the lines in the human hand. I prayed to God that my hand lines wouldn't be all there. In horror, I saw *every single line.*

I wasn't dreaming.

I wanted to scream "NOOO!" but I contained myself, sighed heavily and flopped back onto the carpet. The Rudolph song wasn't even lifting my spirits. It was Christmas, and it was going to be the worst Christmas I ever had in my thirteen years. Well, for starters, I didn't even want to get up. The song switched to *'Jingle Bells.'*

I flopped over on my belly and buried my face in the carpet. After about ten seconds, I gasped and flung myself on my back, still not wanting to get up. I could already feel The Diamond Square vibes closing in on me.

"MERRY CHRISTMAS!" the announcer sang. Everybody in the library groaned, but I groaned the hardest. "EMILY AND MISTRESS SMITH HAVE ARRIVED!" I heard shuffling and I found myself dragging out of the library and down the hall into the Main Room.

This place didn't look the same. The people here had worked hard and fast over the last week and a half. The stairs now had a golden railing (put in by the construction people) and they were less dusty and much shinier. That alone made it look like a whole new staircase; like something that belonged in a mansion.

I had no idea what was going on in our rooms, but it better be good. The floor was mopped and the shining chandelier above us reflected on the tile below. I stared at it, even when I heard a knock, and heard the huge doors opening.

I only looked up when both Mistress Smith and Emily gasped. Right on time, *The Most Wonderful Time of the Year* began piping through the speakers. Emily was wearing a red shirt with snowflakes on it and jeans. Her hair was in the normal huge blonde curls except that she wore a red and white hat on top and a white scarf around her neck. She was wearing grey boots with a little white fluffing at the top.

Emily clasped her gloved hands together and…just kept them there. Mistress Smith's mouth was agape. She was wearing a gray jacket, jeans, boots, a scarf, and a hat.

"This place looks different already!" Emily squealed, twirling around; "who's idea was this?"

"It was a friend of Mrs. Sesmore's" Mr. Waite replied, "but I agreed to the idea. Do come in." Emily and Mistress Smith stepped in slowly, dragging their feet like turtles carefully across the welcome mat…so very slowly. I was thinking- just dust your feet and come in, would you?

"We have so many plans," Mrs. Sesmore said, smiling, "we did buy…" Her face went pale, and there was a silence. Kris and I shared a look. Mrs. Sesmore forced a smile and continued: "We did buy some gifts and we have a…dinner planned."

The woman hadn't even prepared a dinner.

Emily touched her chest, smiled, and nodded. "This is a rather *awkward* time for you to visit," Mrs. Sesmore said and grimaced at all the dust in the air. "We are in the middle of renovation, and the children have had to evacuate to other parts. But they have fully completed the Guest Room since we especially requested that. Please make yourself at home, we'll tell you when gift opening time begins."

Mr. Waite had walked away, in the middle of the conversation. Mistress Smith nodded and guided Emily away. The music stopped. Mrs. Sesmore, all sweaty, turned to us, her plump body looking tired.

"Okay!" she began, "let me lay down the law. We are in the middle of a crisis. We need gifts, wrapped and ready in one hour and a Christmas breakfast ready…NOW! We need a Christmas lunch and most importantly…A CHRISTMAS DINNER!" There was silence.

"Okay," she continued, "let's get through this. Ages 5 to 10, you'll be wrapping presents, putting bows on top and helping wherever else you can. Ten to thirteen, you'll be the ones buying the gifts for both Carson and Emily. I heard there's a fake Santa Claus in the plaza…It's about a mile behind The Diamond Square. Buy some gifts there…14 to 16 you're responsible for making Christmas breakfast, lunch, and DINNER. Ten to thirteen, you can also help with making breakfast before going to the plaza please.

We all looked at her, waiting to see if she would say more. Mrs. Sesmore flung her hands around. "GO! GO! GO!" she screamed, gesturing. I grabbed Kris's hand and fled outside to get some berries. To my surprise, there were none growing. There was barely a tiny branch and a leaf pushing through the dirt. I inspected it closely.

"Is this where you put it?" Kris inquired, kneeling. "When did you plant that?"

"A week and a half ago," I cried despairingly. "It should have grown by now!" I carefully dug around the spot where I had planted the seeds. "What am I gonna tell Mrs. Sesmore now?"

We got up and went inside. I was the one who shared the news with Mrs. Sesmore, and just as I expected, she panicked. She dashed into the kitchen, with Kris and me right behind her. "Okay, everybody!" Mrs. Sesmore announced to the kids shoving each other out of the way, "We have ourselves a problem." Everybody stopped moving to listen.

"You see," Mrs. Sesmore gave everyone eye contact. "We were going to have a berry pie…but now…since we have no berries…" (she made it sound like somebody ate them all or as if it was somebody's fault, but it was really not mine) "we're going to have to use a substitute…which is…noodles."

People started snickering.

"I'm holding my sides!" a boy cried sarcastically, "you're joking, Sesmore. What are we really going to be using?"

"No, we are using noodles," Mrs. Sesmore repeated firmly, approaching the boy, "I am serious."

A girl declared: "It's nice to have a joke and all, but we need to know what we are actually using."

"WE ARE USING NOODLES," Mrs. Sesmore roared, "NOODLES! NOODLES! NOODLES! PEOPLE HAVE USED NOODLES IN PIES SO WHY NOT US? WE PROMISED A PIE TO OUR VISITORS AND IF NOODLES IS THE ONLY THING WE CAN GIVE THEM THEN WE'RE USING NOODLES!" By the time she was finished she was screaming, and everyone was silent once again, looking around.

"And you." Mrs. Sesmore spun around to face me. "You are in so much trouble, so much trouble, missy. So much."

I shuddered. "Hey," Kris came quickly to my defense. "It's not her fault that you forgot to make a pie!" At that moment, there was a gasp and behind us was Emily, with an empty glass in her hand.

Uh-oh.

"I'm so sorry," Emily began.

Nobody said anything. My heart began to beat. I looked at Kris and she looked at me. All eyes were now on Emily, who began backing up, repeating 'I'm so sorry, I'm so sorry' until Mrs. Sesmore perked back to life and found her tongue. "No, no," she muttered, "it's f…fine."

"But I ruined the surprise," moaned Emily, "you were making us a surprise pie."

There was a silence. "I just wanted some water," Emily added, gesturing faintly at the glass. A kid grabbed the glass from Emily, filled it to the brim and passed it back to her. Emily nodded. "Thank you," she said, backing out of the doorway, "and I'm sorry…again." Then she fled, and we could see her go up the stairs to the Guest Room.

There was more silence and now Mrs. Sesmore held a shaky finger up to Kris. "I…you…come with me." She walked towards the doorway, turned around, and gestured for us to come. As we stepped out, some kids 'ooh'-ed at us. "SHUT UP!" Mrs. Sesmore shouted.

We were outside of the kitchen, feeling dazed.

"YOU ARE GOING **OUT!**" screamed Mrs. Sesmore. I looked at the tile and closed my eyes. *No, no, no, no. Not yet. It ain't even spring yet. It's winter, approaching January. We'll freeze on the streets.* There was a faraway crash.

"I **HATE** YOU!" she continued, "and I **HATED** you two since the BEGINNING! If you don't go back where you came from…I'LL FIND A WAY! GET OUT OF MY HOUSE!" She pointed to somewhere else in her house and then briskly walked away to the kitchen.

The library was cold, and we were both bored. The possibility that we would be allowed to go to breakfast, lunch or dinner was extremely low. I, however, could not go without food for more than two hours, and The Diamond Square was testing that fact about me…a lot.

"Okay, Kris, we need a plan," I suggested after a while. I grabbed my notebook which was lying next to the bookshelf (with only two and a half pages filled) and began writing.

Ari and Kris Team Flag

Kris and Ari Team Flag

Ari and Kris Team Flag

TWINS FOREVER **Team Flag**

I wrote, thinking out loud, We should create some mischief. What about while everybody is distracted, we go out and get some food? I'm sure there are some amazing cooks out there. Afterwards, we can sneak back to the library and pretend that nothing happened…

Kristina: Girl, I'm not wasting my day on that. Today's Christmas, and we should get ourselves some pretty gifts! Remember when Mrs. Sesmore said something about getting gifts for Emily? Well, how about we go and buy presents for ourselves! And if anybody asks us, 'Hey, why are you two here?' we can just say we were getting stuff for Emily.

I stopped writing. Kris looked up as if reading my thoughts. "How are we going to get out?" I asked. "Everybody's so caught up in the Christmas Spirit and running around *everywhere*."

Kris tapped my pen on my book for a minute, and then her head snapped back. "You can be the *guard*!" I gave her a stupid blank stare.

Finally, I asked, "I can be what?"

"The guard."

"What does the *guard* in your plan even do?"

"You stay put near the library and signal for me when everything's clear."

"And what do you do?" I stared in dismay as Kris got up, ready to begin her plan. And I was just a measly guard. Kris quickly replied: "When you give me your cue, I'll race out, and then motion you to follow me…when it's safe, of course."

I groaned, reluctantly got up, then froze. "We need a distraction." I began beaming. "Just like in my plan!" Kris impatient, walked around, muttering: "What are we going to do, though?"

I peeked around the doorway. There were a few people walking, but most people were gone or swarming around the kitchen's entrance, looking worried. There was another clang (which we had been hearing lately) and more murmuring…and angry shouting.

"Kris…I think the coast is clear," I whispered. She nodded and commanded me: "Stand guard." I rolled my eyes. Didn't I already "stand guard" for her? A few seconds passed before I motioned for her to go. Kris sprinted off and I followed behind. We tip-toed through the hall and stopped near the Closet Room.

We opened it carefully and searched for thick coats. We put them on quickly. I fluffed my curls out of the hood and zipped up my gray jacket carefully. We closed the huge, dismal door. This was going to be the weirdest part, walking around indoors with the fluffiest coats from the closet.

It was cold inside, but it was still weird to be wearing those coats indoors. Lately, the workload had been increasing, and we had barely seen each other. Just imagine Nathan and Selene. The only time we really saw them was at night, and we would all be in Lalaland as soon as we were on the library rug.

We ducked and hid behind the huge Christmas tree like secret agents. It wasn't necessary, but fun. A few kids were starting to head out, and even though we wanted to be first on Santa's line, we had to blend in as well as we could. Kris opened the door, and I ducked behind her arm. Soon, we were running down the small hill to the plaza, ready to get presents for Christmas!

CHAPTER 18

Fire!

'Rockin' Around the Christmas Tree' was the song playing while we waited for Santa. He was in his festive sleigh, with his red and white uniform. He was a chubby little Santa with white hair and his mustache was lopsided. There were speakers beside his sleigh.

"Well, hey…" Santa said as he caught a glance of us. "There…" he finished, "how are you lovelies doing on Christmas?" He reached into the huge sack at the back of his sleigh and pulled out two presents.

"Good."

"Good."

He nodded. "I reckon you two want a present?" he asked, handing the gifts over to us. Mine was wrapped in Christmas red with a huge white bow. It was medium-sized. Ari's was golden yellow with teddy bear wrapping. It was the biggest present I had seen in a while. "It's nice to see people like you still believing in the Christmas Spirit," Santa bellowed behind us.

We made it back to The Diamond Square before anyone noticed we were gone.

"What did you get?"

"I got this…"

"Oh, *please!*"

"Uh, really?" I held up my new furry teddy bear, that was wearing a school dress. It came with a fountain pen and the smallest writing book I'd ever seen (with no lines).

"At least you can use that!" Ari snapped, looking at her own gift. It was a pink toddler's play bike. There were a bunch of rainbow buttons which either played the ABCs, numbers from 1-10 or "sleep-time".

I fingered the little bike before looking back at my teddy. I sighed. This hadn't been what I expected or wanted. Before we had a chance to put away the toys Selene and Nathan burst in through the doors.

"Where have you guys been?" Selene demanded. I attempted to smile. Lying wasn't even necessary at this point. "Mrs. Sesmore has been searching EVERYWHERE to punish you guys!" Selene exclaimed, "where were you?" She noticed our presents and covered her mouth. I tried to hide my teddy by leaning back on it, but what happened next is the reason why I hate teddy bears to this very day.

"Let's spell cat! C-A-T."

Apparently, my teddy bear seemed to be able to talk. I froze, desperately trying to move my legs, but they stayed on the ground like hardened cement. I heard steps coming down the hallway.

The rest of Christmas was a blur of Emily and Mistress Smith, tasting our noodle pie (it was horrible) and unwrapping gifts. It was *definitely* a funny Christmas and that's a pretty big thing to say (especially here).

The sounds of an alarm filled the room. I screamed and covered my ears. Everyone else was shouting and squealing. In my terror, I bumped into a bookshelf and screamed again, the alarm petrifying me.

The announcer buzzed loudly: "Well, it seems that SOMEBODY'S cooking did not go well! Children, the fire alarm is sounding and due to technical difficulties, other alarms have malfunctioned to increase the sound. We suspect the fire is from the kitchen so children, please evacuate safely outside and avoid that area!"

I, along with Ari, Selene, Nathan, and five other children squabbled through the door, trying to get out all at once. The lights were off, and the eerie red of the sirens made me want to leave, as quickly as possible.

I tore my way through the hallways, noticing that both the sirens' screams were getting louder. The door at the exit creaked as the guard took out the keys to let us go outside. I was getting lost behind the Christmas tree and almost fell into the dead fireplace. The moonlight coming through the doors were like the key to Heaven.

I scrambled into the outdoors, instantly freezing. I didn't even think of grabbing a coat. I began to shiver, my knees knocking together. I had to go back in there and get myself a coat or I might just get severe hypothermia.

The alarms weren't as loud out here and that was part of the reason why I was reluctant to go back inside. Besides, people were still screaming, grunting, and groaning. I prayed to God for the courage, braced myself, and then sprinted back through the cracked open main doors.

I felt my way with my hands down the hall until I found a crowd of kids clamoring around a door. I fumbled it open with the help of somebody else and the jackets poured out like an avalanche. I made my way to the closet, swiped the first coat I saw and sprinted back into the Main Room and back to the safety of the outdoors.

Fumbling into my jacket I breathed a sigh of relief. The alarms had shut off and my head had stopped spinning, but kids were still screaming and crying and frightened. What was going on in there?

A girl collapsed at the door and pounded it with her little fist. "LET US IN!" she screamed, and then turned to us, "What's going on in there?"

I couldn't believe people wanted to go back to The Diamond Square after what had just happened. Were their ears and eyes immune to the danger?

The kids continued talking but most of the time I couldn't tell who was chatting.

"I thought it was safe here!"

"Yeah! Me too!"

"I want my mommy, but she's gone forever!" sobbed a little girl.

"Hush don't cry!" the only maid out here cried. She had pinned up her brown hair in a bun, and although she was tall, she wore heels. "You'll cause the others to panic."

In other words: "You'll lead The Thing right to us!"

"Do you think we're gonna be okay?" a little boy asked. Another girl went up to the doorway and screamed: "HEY, YA'LL ARE GONNA DIE!"

Everyone was questioning the maid, asking her what was going on and why the gates were shut. Why was there groaning? The alarms had been shut off, so why were people still screaming? Someone started a rumor about a monster.

"Bestie," someone whispered loudly, "remember the thing we saw the other night when we were exploring in the nearby woods? Do you think that could be the monster?"

A girl with short hair kept on disturbing the maid, asking her repeatedly what was wrong. Finally, she bit her lip and nervously announced with a heavy accent: "She is not listening!"

"We can't stay here all night!" I shouted. The maid stood there, clutching some keys. She could open the door! The crowd pushed in trying to grab the keys, but the maid kept them clutched in her grasp. We stepped back at the sound of loud, low grunting and more shouting.

"LET US IN!" a small voice shouted from the other side of the door. Suddenly, the maid turned pale and then fell over.

There was silence and the panic intensified. How can this be getting any more intense than it already was?

"The maid has fainted!"

"What are we going to do?"

"The big question really is, did she hit her head?"

"I don't think so. "She fell on the grass."

"Our only protector is down!"

Quicker than a flash, flames poured out of the windows and the smoke waved out. The fire was spreading and if it wasn't extinguished soon, The Diamond Square would burn and fall on the children and adults still trapped inside which included Emily and Mistress Smith!

The flames grew, and I shivered, afraid that the glass would explode. A girl pounded at the gate and screamed: "My cousin is in the kitchen! He'll die!"

A teen knelt beside her and unsympathetically remarked: "Well, I hope you've had a last loving memory with him because, sweetie, he's dead." The frightened girl began sobbing loudly. Commotion was everywhere. Usually, I'd be cruising in a crowd, talking, but not now.

Someone opened and closed a door. Everyone crowded around the people who were attempting to aid the nurse.

At last, the fire was brought under control and the sparks terrorizing both the windows and me died away.

It was the crack of dawn, and we stood at attention. For the third time, Mr. Waite asked loudly who set the kitchen on fire. At first, he immediately believed Ari and I did this, until a kid (bless his heart, we owe him one) claimed that he saw us outside which proved that we didn't cause it.

We found out that the 'monster' was just a male servant groaning in his sleep.

"Okay, then." Mr. Waite strolled back and forth, a threatening stick in his hand. "If nobody steps forward, everybody in this place will be put out." There was a huge gasp and the children looked at one another as if to say, "Hey did *you* do it? C'mon, tell!"

After a few minutes of whispering and murmuring a girl stepped forward. She was short and had a single braid in her hair. She claimed that she knew who set the kitchen on fire.

"It was all some sort of accident," she began. "We were sleeping in the kitchen as usual, and my best friend, Swirl, thought it was so stinky because of the leftover smells from Christmas. So, she sneaked into Mrs. Sesmore's room, grabbed a peppermint-scented candle, lit it, and brought it to the kitchen. I didn't know she had done this till we were outside. Swirl sleeps close to a curtain so she had been planning on blowing it out before she went to bed, but she dozed off before she could.

"Once she saw the fire, she sprinted from the spot to avoid being seen, I guess." She stepped back into the crowd, giving a nod to an invisible somebody. We were all silent as Swirl stepped forward, got beaten and was escorted outside of the doors of The Diamond Square.

That little troublemaker. I'm jealous.

CHAPTER 19

Big Decision

"I wonder what it's going to look like," Selene exclaimed, covering her eyes. We, The Diamond Square Gang, (Selene, Nathan, Kris and I were outside The Diamond Square, standing before the huge door. We really wanted to see how the place had improved. It was freezing, even with our jackets on, and I wanted to get inside before I caught a severe case of the common cold. Selene was nervous.

"If I go in, and it isn't nice I'll feel so disappointed," she announced. "But I don't want to keep on imagining so that when I do go in, I don't see much of what I really wanted."

"F…fine," Kris remarked, "if you w…won't go in, I will." She attempted to push open the door. Selene uncovered her face and squealed: "Okay, okay, fine! I want to see it too!" We all pushed open the door and our eyes bulged out at the new, beautiful sight.

The floor was all marble, and the chandelier seemed bigger and was so bright you could barely look at it. The two staircases looked the same (except for the 'gold' railings). All at once we began racing to our dormitory. Nathan arrived first and flung open the door like a madman.

Our eyes got wide again, and not in an I've-just-seen-something-amazing way. The two extra beds were claimed by two energetic toddlers, a girl and a boy. They were giggling and jumping up and down. We stopped in our tracks, watching the unwelcome aliens who had just invaded our private space.

The children looked at us with sideways glances, and then they grinned. Nathan slammed the door shut and then turned to us.

"I'm not sharing a dorm with anybody, under eight" he informed us.

"Okay, people," whispered Kris, "what we have to do now is slowly walk away from here and find somebody else's dorm. Half of the people here are newcomers and are randomly claiming dorms anyway."

We all agreed to walk away and went inside a dorm that looked nice and homey enough. We settled in and took a bed each. No matter what, we were going to have two other extra people in this room, or any room we moved into. Looking around and settling in, I realized that I had forgotten something.

"I left my book and pen at the library!" I told them. "I'll be right back!"

"You'd better not be late when the breakfast and chore bells ring!" Selene called after me. I raced through the hallway and down the stairs. Everything looked so clean and inviting. I quickly grabbed my book and pen out of the library. Marveling at everything, I was so busy staring that I stumbled right into Carson.

I apologized and left. I sprinted up the stairs faster than I had come down them, anxious to get to our new dorm, get ready for showers and our little learning session that was now only once a week. I made it just in time for the new breakfast bell to sound. After breakfast, we headed past the library to learn.

The classroom that once held rows and rows of boring brown tables with chairs was now a completely different place.

There were actual school tables like the ones we had at our last school before we came to The Diamond Square. There were two chairs at every table and there was a little slot to put our things in, not that we had any stuff to put in there. At Mrs. Sesmore's nook the chalkboard was replaced by a whiteboard with four different colored markers on her desk along with a ruler and a mug. If only those renovation people knew what that ruler was really going to be used for.

I sat down at the table next to Kris. Our seats were just in front of a white boarded window. This place really was giving off a whole new fresh air. While Mrs. Sesmore was looking around The Diamond Square to see if anybody was skipping 'school' (they would have a sound whipping and no breakfast) I opened my journal and flipped through the pages.

Tucked between the pages of my journal, I discovered a note from Carson:

I need to tell you something.

Come to the bridge in the plaza.

Come after everybody's asleep (11:50-midnight).

DO NOT TELL ANYBODY ABOUT THIS!!!
(In fact, eat this or burn it with fire!!!)

-Carson

The Diamond Square didn't look so pretty at night. The guards at the front door made me want to go back to sleep. I decided to escape the way I usually did when it came to getting to the bridge.

I sprinted as fast as I could through the yard and over the gate and ran down the hill. When I came to the plaza, I went on the bridge the easy way, by climbing the stairs wedged between two buildings. Carson was already there, and I stepped toward him hesitantly.

"Well, hello there." Carson swished around on the glass bottom. I sat down as well, looking around, fearing being kidnapped. This was the first time I had felt scared or jumpy on the bridge. It was usually the other way around.

I didn't comment and waited for him to say what he wanted to say so I could go back to my dorm and sleep. I hadn't had an ounce of rest so far tonight.

"Okay," Carson began, "do you want me to cut straight to the point or explain this thoroughly?"

"Just straight to the point."

"Thank God. Anyway, how do you feel about The Diamond Square so far?"

"I mean, the changes have been nice so far, but not so much in other ways."

"Like what?"

"Well, let's see," I replied irritably, "I'm ravenously hungry, tired, and I have this weird slow, mushy, sad feeling. And every single night I dream about HOME!" I slapped the side of the bridge with the last word.

"I can tell you're sick and tired of this place," Carson said, way too casually.

"More than sick and tired."

"Well, then." Carson spoke in a deep and mysterious voice, then looked around a little. My hands fidgeted in my lap.

I stayed silent, looking straight into Carson's eyes. Most of the time his eyes looked teal blue, but now I knew. Oh boy, those eyes were as gray as steel. I shifted, feeling uncomfortable beyond words.

Just say it, just say it.

The seconds felt like hours, and I could feel my heart beating rapidly. I began to sweat with anticipation. Finally, Carson finished nonchalantly:

"…to leave."

For a second, I froze, looking at him, trying to figure out what type of joke this was. "What do you mean 'to leave?'" I asked dubiously. "I'm glad you asked," Carson replied, "as you may well know, my dad used to run this place where people lived, and worked a lot, but now it has become an orphanage.

So, annually, I pick one person--usually a child, because adults here WANT to stay-and that one certain person is given a train ticket…" He pulled a little piece of paper out of his pocket and gave it to me. "…And they use the train ticket to escape. For people who still have loved ones alive they can contact them, or if they don't, they can just go into an orphanage where people actually care about them.

"So, you're just going to use this ticket to get your behind out of here." I pictured myself strutting my way out of The Diamond Square. Oh yes, back to Aunt Maybelle, ice cream, more food, pampering…Wait, no…no…it couldn't be that easy.

Before I could tell Carson this though, he added: "Oh! And I'll let you in on another little secret. Did you know Emily used to be here? She was actually the latest person, before you, that I gave a ticket to."

"So why is she still coming back here? Does she really love this place?"

Carson shrugged. "She's a brave chick," he said, "my dad knows that at any moment, if they mistreat her, she can go to the local news, tattletale and then this place would be shut down. Mistress Smith is her aunt or older cousin or something. For most people I give this option to, in two weeks they're on that train and I never hear from them again. But she's different."

"Do you get in trouble?"

"Only for Emily," Carson replied, "but the others snuck out and my dad didn't even notice."

A smile crept onto my face. "Where's the other one?" This was probably the beginning of a new beginning. Another chance, another redo, surely.

"What other one?" Carson asked. *What other one? What does he mean what other one?* I told him I meant the other ticket for Kris. I wasn't leaving without her.

"Well," Carson said, getting up. "Then I guess you have yourself a problem. Goodnight!"

How could he be so? I must choose between my own twin sister and freedom! And he just has the audacity to get up and leave like I was deciding whether I wanted chicken or turkey for dinner. Of course, I realized, it was obvious that as an only child, Carson never had these types of problems.

After a while of thinking and staring at the moon, I decided I better go back to The Diamond Square and think about everything that I would have to decide on in two weeks' time.

Smoke weaved its way from the train and into the sky where it disappeared. I had checked everything several times, yet something was missing. Train ticket, book, and pen. Something was still missing, but what?

"Last chance, young lady," the train driver snapped at me, "either you're coming or not. I ain't got the time for games." I took a deep breath and boarded the train just as it pulled off from the station.

Sitting down on a red seat next to the window, I looked at the landscape as we passed by. I opened my book to write about everything when a picture escaped from a page and fluttered to the floor.

I took it up cautiously. It looked fragile. It was a picture of two girls working at the Moody Moon. Me and…

"KRIS!" I shouted out loud. Heads turned my way. I jumped out of my seat and sprinted to the train driver's compartment. I held him by the shoulder, much to his annoyance and disgust and screamed: "Stop the train!!! Please stop this train!!!"

The train driver told me to get to my seat before I got myself into problems. Reluctantly, after what seemed like an hour of begging I sagged into my seat with my head down.

Before I could do anything else, Kris appeared outside of the window, just standing there, looking at me through disappointed eyes.

I scrolled down the window. "It's not my fault!!!" I screamed out of it, "I knew there was something missing."

Kristina's eyes seemed excessively big at that moment. She didn't say anything back to me. Just stared at me one last time and walked away.

"Ari!" Kris whispered loudly, peeking over my shoulder. I lifted my head, getting out of my daydreams. We were in the classroom, and one of the male servants was teaching algebra. Seeing Kris trying to read what I had written I slapped my notebook shut.

"What *is* your problem?" I asked her, trying to sound angry. I knew I was being harsh, but I didn't want to tell Kris about the ticket business right now.

"Chill, I need to tell you something," Kris informed me. "Selene's friend's friend, told Selene's friend, who told Selene, who told me what I am telling you: that she overhead Mrs. Sesmore saying to one of the maids we're going to have a spoonful of either *rice* or *MEAT*."

My problems dissolved immediately. "M…meat?" I couldn't believe my ears. We hadn't had meat for…forever!

Ever since more and more kids started arriving, we had less and less food, more misery, and more chores (but that was the least of our problems). In two days' time, it would be New Year's Day…. January. It just gave me even more nightmares thinking about it. At night now, we were freezing, and our thin blankets weren't helping much. Last night, Kris and I tried to squeeze ourselves between our mattresses and our bed at an angle so that we could breathe, but that didn't work.

It was evening, and only Kris and I were in our dorms. Kris was doodling on the walls with her fingers, and I was trying to read a book I had found in The Diamond Square library, which was probably the least renovated place. Every time I would read a paragraph or two, I would start thinking about something else and then have to read it all over again.

I swapped books with my notebook and wrote:

Why do I think about a decision when I already know what my choice will be? It's obvious. I know I won't leave, and I'll stay with Kris, but the other side of me just wants to go. I don't want to deal with this winter.

I don't want to make this decision!

~Ari~

"What decision?" Kristina was standing right behind me and had read my entire entry. What does a girl have to do to get some PRIVACY around here?

I began searching my brain for an excuse, but it just went blank. In the end, I blurted out: "It's a fiction story I'm writing."

"Ya, but…" Kris collapsed back on her bed. "If it's a fiction story, why do you have our names in it?"

"I don't have my name in it."

"You signed it, though!" Kris protested.

I sighed, running out of excuses. "Well," I muttered wearily, "fiction stories can have real-life characters as well."

Kris was staring at me. I knew she wasn't buying a thing I was saying to her. I fixed myself on my pillow. The time had officially come for me to tell the truth about what happened on the bridge. I took a deep breath and started.

"Kris…I have to tell you something."

CHAPTER 20

Flashback

"I think you should leave!" Nathan declared. We were all in our new dormitory. The walls were beige, and the flooring was a snow-white tile. Our beds were the same but with red pillows and covers. Halfway into what Ari was telling me, Selene and Nathan burst in. Now, we were having a Diamond Square Gang meeting. It was almost 9 PM now.

I shot him a 'seriously?' look. "Hmph!" I grunted. Nathan shrugged. "I mean, it makes sense," he plodded on, still thinking his opinion was better. "I mean, staying here with Selene or going to live with a nice relative? Ha! Hasta la vista, Selene!"

Selene scoffed and turned her head away. "Hmph!" Nathan looked at her and shrugged again unsympathetically. Ari twitched in her bed.

"Are you guys family?" I asked them. This was a question I had been thinking of asking since I met them.

"Cousins," they chimed.

"So, don't you two mean *anything* to each other?" Ari probed. Whether she was trying to make a point or was just asking a random question I didn't know.

There was a brief silence until Nathan asked what she meant. "What I mean is, um…" Ari twiddled her fingers around. "Don't you guys love each other….?"

They both nodded.

"What I meant is, do you love each other enough to make a big sacrifice?" Ari urged on.

There was silence.

"I was just joking," Nathan said softly after the pause. Selene nodded as if she were controlled by something. The lamp light on a small table in a corner added to the uncomfortable silence. I could hear footsteps coming down the hall and the opening and closing of doors. Nathan popped up and whispered: "Sesmore's coming." Being closest to the lamp, I popped up, and turned it off. Immediately the room went completely dark, with only one window of moonlight pouring in. We settled into bed, covers up to our chins, not moving, trying to pretend we had been asleep for hours.

I heard the door creak open. My eyes really wanted to open but I kept them squeezed shut until I heard Mrs. Sesmore close the door again. Once Mrs. Sesmore was two doors down Nathan murmured: "I think it's better to go to sleep now."

"'Night, Diamond Square Gang," Selene breathed.

"'Night."

"'Night."

"'Night."

Looking at the clock with the moonlight's help, I could tell it was now 10:40 P.M. I tossed about, my blanket strangling me. I couldn't sleep. Ari had gone to bed twenty minutes ago, but I couldn't close my eyes without having to open them again. I needed to be satisfied.

As quietly as a mouse, I broke free from my covers and crept over to Ari's bedside. Shivering, I grabbed her diary and slowly opened the door. The darkness was accompanied by nothing but snoring. I had planned to try and sneak somewhere where there was light (maybe the library) that wasn't my dorm so no one would wake up and ask me what I was doing. One peak at the guards and I closed the door back. I was just going to have to risk it for the biscuit.

I flipped the lamp on and opened the book. According to the first date, Ari had started this book on the first day of the seventh grade. Half of me wanted to go from page one to the latest entry. I mean, what other chance would I have to read my sister's personal thoughts?

I shook my head. I would do that later, after I was one thousand percent sure that my twin sister would not leave me here in exchange for her freedom.

I found out what happened on the bridge, through some of the dialogue. and something I found was familiar. I remembered earlier in class when Ari was writing, and I managed to see: "

...appeared in front of my eyes. Outside of the window."

I knew she had to be referring to something or someone, but I didn't know that thing or person was me! I didn't find anything comforting either. Sure, she had some words saying she couldn't possibly leave me here, but there was still that uncertainty.

... Ugh, why couldn't there be TWO TICKETS?!?

...Why do I have to make this decision?

Girl, if you aren't leaving me, why can't you just *SAY* that? I flipped to other pages, smiling at some things, but the fact that the girl I had known for thirteen years might abandon me made me close the book and climb into bed. I reluctantly lay down and fell asleep.

The hall was longer and darker than it was supposed to be. My feet should have been on the ground hours ago. Now all I saw was black and Ari leading the way. At first, I had been the one leading, but hesitance made me drop behind.

We were pranking our math teacher, Mr. Henio, but it was taking an unexpected turn...

The trail ended in two different paths. One clearly stated, 'Kris' and the other, 'Ari.' Ari and I exchanged looks. I took a step back. "C'mon," Ari urged, "don't you want to see Mr. Henio's face when he's sprayed with ketchup?"

I looked at the path, pictured his face, nodded, and then walked as quickly as I could through the tunnel. I could see the light and Ari waiting for me on the other end. Before I could reach her, however, I dropped my bottle of ketchup and tripped over it. I plummeted into an unseen bottomless pit, screaming; my arms and legs flailing.

Orange, yellow, and pink clouds were rolling around in the sky. A huge yellow and orange ball of light began reaching outwards without being invited. The clouds didn't seem to mind it, they just covered it bleakly, trying to move on with their day. At least they could move on.

The grass would probably be the color of lime if it weren't covered with a blanket of snow. If we were outside there would probably be a few speckles of black and brown because our clothes were so ragged and icky, literally swallowing us from the neck down, so that we practically looked like blobs running around, trying to avoid being spanked or thrown out.

The snow was lightly falling from the sky. I was observing everything happening from the small window in the library. Today, I was actually dusting books and furniture and sweeping the floors. It seemed to me that every five minutes or so, a maid would check to make sure I wasn't doing anything else but cleaning. Other maids were checking other places. This place had no privacy, the food never satisfied me, and the unbearable cold was making my fingernails blue. The other day I had gotten moderate hypothermia and had to sit in front of the fireplace with a bunch of other desperate kids.

It had been eight days since Ari had gotten her invitation from Carson, seven days since she told me, and day six of the Official Twin Sister "Fight." It wasn't exactly a fight, but we weren't as close as we usually are.

It went like this: If Ari and I passed each other in the hallways, we would just nod. No smile or wave, just a tiny little nod. We wouldn't speak to each other much, but it wasn't like we were refusing to do so. As usual, we would sit next to each other in class, but not talk or giggle or anything like that. Ari would completely turn her body away from me or use some other system so I couldn't see a word she was writing in her diary. She didn't even trust me. Sometimes we would sit next to each other in the lunchroom, but most of the time, when possible, we would sit away from each other.

It had only been happening for six days, but it felt like years had gone by. Anyway, in the meantime, I was going to stand in the library wondering how my life turned out this way.

As I was dusting, a book fell off the bookshelf and landed on the floor. I picked it up slowly. It was big and had a lot of pages. I've seen books with a lot of pages, but I brushed the layer of dust off the cover and read the title:

Worldly Facts:

Greater Generations

Hawley Slim

I had seen this before. I opened the book eagerly and began reading it.

Chapter 1:

Why be lied to?

Every day we face life's challenges.

And sometimes, we don't know how to.

Yet, the laws of life are running in.

front of your eyes, and you.

neglect it, regret it. "It's too hard."

The Keys to Life are essential.

And never to be misused.

I knew the next bit all too well. Too well.

BE HONEST!
"Nobody believes a liar, even when she is telling the truth."
Even the littlest lies, the ones we call "white" can cost a fortune.
BE CONNECTED!
Friends, family, teachers, random people, the world is supposed to connect. Stay at the side of a person who doesn't have it easy. Talking to people relieves some forms of depression and stress. A little talk can take a huge weight off somebody else's shoulders.
SHOW HUMILITY!
"Whoever wants to be first, must be last of all and servant of all. If-.....

Something caught my eye. At the bottom of the page something was written there. My eyes filled with tears automatically as I read and reread what was there. No, it wasn't true. I rubbed my eyes, tears wetting the book. I opened them again.

I hope and pray that my blessed and talented little girls, Kristina, and Ariel grow up to be strong, determined, honest, humble, kind little women, even after we are not here.
God Bless,
Helene and Turman Collins.

"What is wrong with you?" The maid who had been checking on me was at the door. "Why are you sitting on the floor, reading a book? You're supposed to be doing your chores! Get up and get a move on!"

I stayed on the ground and shifted a little. The maid put her hands on her hips. "I'm going to count to ten," she said just beyond a whisper. "And if you're not up with that book out of your hands by then I will *give* you a reason to cry. One…Two…Three…Four…"

Time was ticking, but I couldn't stop myself from rereading the little message at the bottom of the page. How did The Diamond Square get our book? Dad and Mom always used to read a chapter to us at bedtime or whenever we wanted them to. So, who came in and grabbed the book from our bookshelf and brought it here?

"Eight…Nine…." I slammed the book closed, sprang up, put the book back on the shelf, and dried my tears. The maid crossed her arms and shook her head. "You better hope I'm not serving food this evening," she remarked feisty-like, "acting all sassy 'round me." She turned around and strutted out of the room.

Bye-bye.

"But I betrayed their trust!" I bellowed. I was in Selene's bed, and she was trying unsuccessfully to make me feel better. But as sure as the Mississippi River exists, I wasn't gonna be feeling better any time soon.

"I mean, everybody makes mistakes," Selene reasoned. "Like, you.

guys haven't been honest for a few weeks, big deal. NO! It's not okay! But, well…"

"We haven't been lying for just a few weeks." We really started getting into this lying thing since we were seven and our parents died, but it really heated up after we moved in with our aunt.

"What are you talking about, Kris?" Selene cut me off.

"It's complicated," I muttered, "you don't need to know." At this point Ari came in, closed the door, and declared: "Nathan's in juvenile court, he…" When she spotted me, she nodded. At this, Selene and I began hysterically laughing. Ari joined in as well.

"Is Nate really in juvenile court?" Selene asked dubiously.

"No, that was a metaphor," Ari replied, "but it looks like that, though. Somebody ate the New Year's cupcakes. An engaged couple that Mrs. Sesmore had known since high school is coming on New Year's Eve to count down. They were supposed to be for them. Four other kids besides Nathan are on 'trial'."

Selene told us that earlier today she had devised a plan about The Leaving Situation. We sat down and she began telling us what she was thinking.

Why Selene's idea won't work.

☐ On Christmas day Ari and I made an oath to never cause trouble in The Diamond Square ever again. Just leaving, without permission would be causing problems. From December 25th, our New Year's resolution was to become better people.

☐ *It's really just...crazy. The idea is nuts, or is Selene the one who's nuts?*

A Christmas song is playing, faster and more tragically than it should be. I'm in The Diamond Square, in the middle of a tile, twirling. Oh, no, now I'm not; now I'm running away from Mrs. Sesmore and Mr. Waite. Wait, is that FIRE?! I hop on a moving orange car, narrowly dodging a whole rake.

I make it into a city that's full of people. Nobody takes heed of the crazy girl on the car. Suddenly, the driver spots me and frightened, jerks the car which makes me fly off. I tumble into a dark tunnel. I always seem to be coming off badly in my dreams.

2:13 AM. I had been up for at least forty-five minutes. It seemed as if it was snowing in here. You can't really sleep when everything around you is literally ice. I rolled over, away from the window. Now I was looking at all four of us, myself, Ari, Selene, Nathan (I don't remember when he came in). In six more days, everything in my life could change.

Or everything could terribly, horribly stay the same.

CHAPTER 21

Jailbreak

For somebody who doesn't know what's going on, I'm quite sure I'm handling this situation well. The apartment was in flames, but I'm sure I've experienced that before. I found the fire extinguisher and struggled to get it to work. One blast comes out of the nozzle and hits both my face and the wall behind me. I turn it around and I am about to start spraying when I fall down and lose the extinguisher. Flames are creeping up towards me and I scream.

Out of the corner of my eyes, I see that Kris is on the balcony, dangling dangerously above the ground, which is like MILLIONS of miles away. One look out of the window and I'm pretty frightened when I see nothing but clouds below.

Just when I think it's happening too fast, something appears beside me. It looks like a human, but…

"Hello," the thing says, "my name is Carson, and I am your genie. You have one wish, and you have to use it in a one-minute time frame that's…"

"Save me and help Kris," I demand. The Carson Genie makes an idiotic face. "One wish," it repeats.

"What do you mean?"

"Who are you saving, madam?" Silence. I struggle to get up, but the pain makes me fall back down. The floor is crumbling. "I DON'T KNOW. JUST DO SOMETHING!" I scream.

A rubber chicken appears on the floor. The balcony breaks and Kristina falls, screaming. Ignoring the pain, I sprint …

January 1st

Two days. I have two days. In two days, my entire life may change, and in two days, nothing may happen at all. Lately, I've been having the same genie dream and every time I take too long to make a wish, a rubber chicken, a live duck, a book, and even a tablet appeared once, and the genie kept on making this idiotic face. One time I socked him, but that time I fell as well.

Selene's plan was like this. We would leave early in the morning and find some form of transportation throughout the city. But consider this, Selene thought all of us—the whole Diamond Square Gang--should go as well.

Even though I know I'm not going, someone else is telling me that I should go. I'm carrying an empty, heavy gray bucket when I cross paths with Carson. I stopped him right in his tracks and demanded the tickets.

"What do you mean "the tickets"?" Carson asked in exasperation. "There's only **ONE** ticket, and that is singular, for your information."

"I know you have more than one," I responded. "If you gave two to Emily and Mistress Smith, you could give four to me." I stopped, and then added: "I mean at least two?"

"They're sold out!" Carson exclaimed. "I have no more. NO MORE. Are you deaf or crazy?"

"Are there really no more tickets, anywhere, in the world?" I interrogated in pure desperation. I was at the point that if there were any spare tickets in Australia, I guess I was going to have to pop down there.

Carson looked at me and crossed his arms, with something close to a smile on his face. He invited me to follow him to his room.

Carson went onto the Chrome tab and typed something into the search bar. His room was big and had a huge blue and white bed. The windows were shut, and he had a fireplace going and a little heater besides. It reminded me of a tropical island. I felt like frozen food that had just been taken out of a freezer and was now thawing. I didn't want to leave here, ever. After a moment of waiting, a website appeared on the screen, it's theme orange and white. He scrolled down just a little bit and clicked on a headline.

The headline was written in bold letters: **GANGSTERS CAUGHT ON THE RUN.** I brushed his hand away and began scrolling down. I hadn't been on an electronic device for such a long time, I felt as if I had to do the honors of going down the page.

Yesterday the Police Station got a call at 3:30 in the afternoon about eight suspicious men who were trying to board a train. The train was not allowed to leave until the police arrived, much to the annoyance of the passengers on board. When the police arrived to investigate, the suspects fled. The criminals were chased and had to surrender the tickets. When returned, it was found that the tickets were stolen...

Blah, blah, blah.

After much discussion, the officers decided that for safekeeping it was best to keep the tickets at their station. "We want to ensure that train safety continues," the chief said when interviewed. "We will keep the tickets here and we will not use them."

NEXT STORY: LOCAL WOMAN CALLS 9-1-1 to help get rubber band out of hair...

I closed the tab and raised my arms in exasperation. "So, you're telling me that the only tickets in this world for this particular train are here at our local police station?" I queried. "Thanks a lot, big help."

"Hey, don't get mad at me." Carson slapped his laptop closed. "I'm not the one who asked about train tickets."

"I'm NOT breaking into a police station and stealing those tickets!" I cried, crossing my arms.

"And I never said you had to," Carson replied slowly.

Uh-oh.

"But if you pay for it, it's not stealing, right?" he continued, pacing around, thinking. "You can go there, buy the tickets, and then we have no problems."

If I paid for the tickets, that meant I wasn't going to be in trouble, right? I mean, you technically aren't stealing if you pay for something.

"I'll have to think about it," I murmured, and left the room.

Steal- to take another person's property without permission or legal right and without intending to return it.

E.g.: The boy <u>stole</u> the little girl's five dollars and quickly stashed it in his pocket.

I still felt like it was stealing. Nothing in the definition had anything to do with payment or money. I closed the dictionary and put it back on the shelf. The bucket was waiting for me in the doorway. I still hadn't used it to clean the floor. I went outside to use the garden tap. Kristina was there, cleaning the outside of the windows. We didn't say a word to each other.

Hurriedly, I rushed back inside and used the soap from the stinky, dirty, and disgusting bathroom we orphans used to make the water bubbly. The bathroom would be the last place I would clean.

I began doing the floor in the Hall where guests, Mrs. Sesmore, Mr. Waite, and Carson eat. The Main Room would be too difficult to clean now.

I am flailing. All I can see are purple and pink clouds and then the figures of people floating by me…the genie and another girl. They gave me a choice once again to save myself or Kris.

Before I can answer, I see the open window in a police station, I go over to it and go inside. Kristina is in there. I took something off a desk when several police officers came rushing in. They locked us in jail even though we are minors and should be accompanied by an adult. I bang on the poles, anxious to get out and escape. "HELP!!!

The room was dark, and it was silent except for some rustling and the occasional banging from next door. I got out from under my covers, passed Kris's bed and turned on the lamp. More rustling.

"Morning, Diamond Square Gang," I whispered. There was a little bit of shuffling as my dormmates got up.

Finally, Selene moaned: "W…what time is it?"

"I don't know," I responded honestly, "but I need to tell you something, I…"

"C'mon, you can't interrupt somebody's good night's sleep," Kris complained.

"Yeah, I know," I continued, "but I have to tell you guys something. It has to do with the ticket."

The grumpiness of the atmosphere wore off and I now had everybody's attention. I could see all of them clearly, and all their anticipation was making them fidget.

"So, I was doing my chores…"

Carson told his dad and Mrs. Sesmore that Nathan, Selene, Kris, and I would be cleaning his bedroom besides our regular chores, but instead we were busy making our plans. It made me nervous to know that tomorrow we would be heading out from The Diamond Square, hopefully, forever.

The Plan

We leave around 5:45 in the morning, which is usually the time we get up and start our chores. This evening we're supposed to pack everything (as if we have anything to pack) for the trip tomorrow.

Carson has saved some money which we will all spend on the following:

☐ *The tickets at the police station*

□ *Food*

□ *Extras maybe?*

(Carson is coming with us for the sake of getting away for a few moments. He's not going to run away like the rest of us.)

I'm scared.

Kris's and my plan: We have two choices: see whether Axel or Aunt Maybelle will help us out. But we sent that letter to our aunt so long ago.

Lunch was a talkative event. Everybody was talking and blabbering about who they wanted to live with, what food they would order, and all that other stuff. We basically had a whole day of no tasks thanks to Carson. Even though we only had a half slice of bread and a few grapes, this would be the last day we would be eating like this, so we wolfed it down. Everybody, even Selene who had once tried to throw a mop at him, had to admit she probably "misjudged him." Meaning Carson.

And me?

I knew he was a good guy from the start.

The Thanksgiving table was lively. Seven-year-old me asked Dad if he could pass the gravy. Dad replied: "Gladly," and presented the white bowl as if it were gold. Without hesitation I poured it all over my rice, until our pet parrot flew over, stuck his beak into it, and slurped it happily.

We all burst into applause. After dinner, Mom and Dad told Kris and me to stay behind. Dad took my hands in his, and Mom took Kris's. I could never forget that moment; I would need it for later.

"We always want you to stay out of trouble," Dad had announced quietly, "That's the one thing we want you to always try to do…. stay out of trouble. However," (followed

by a very long silence) "When Life gives you opportunities, it's always the best decision to reach out and grab them, or else lose everything in the end."

Even with my eyelids closed, I knew it was time to go. It was a strong feeling. My heart automatically began to beat faster. As I slowly opened my eyes, one word kept repeating itself in my mind. Revolution. Revolution. Revolution.

I had searched for the meaning yesterday:

Definition 3: Revolution-- A sudden, or complete, change.

This day of my life was the best definition of revolution if you asked me. Despite the fact, however, I was terrified to start this amazing, perfect day.

The door creaked open, and somebody said: "People are gonna be up in ten minutes, let's go!" I rolled over. Carson was standing in the doorway, fully dressed and prepared. A stack of the greens was in his hand and a camera was around his neck.

Once everyone was awake, there was a huge commotion. I quickly grabbed my journal and pen and froze. The cover of the book was a pastel galaxy with white outlined letters lined with silver. If you had flipped through the pages and not read any of them, you would think Ari Collins was a normal girl living a normal life.

I was about twenty to thirty pages before the end. Maybe the rest would be about me having a ball, the time of my life in school or in Aunt Maybelle's apartment.

If she still wanted us.

"C'mon, let's go!" Selene urged when she saw I had taken my pen out and was flipping pages.

"One sec." I quickly found the next blank page and wrote:

"When Life gives you opportunities, it's always the best decision to reach out and grab them or lose everything in the end."

When I was finished, we dashed out of our room, not even bothering to do anything to it. We would never come back. We crept down the stairs and Carson got five jackets for us to wear. Then we opened the back door. I was probably the only one who took a last look before dashing outside.

We took wide strides across the garden. Despite the fact it was frozen over with snow and ice, it looked much better than it had when Kris and I first came here.

Maybe it was green, a long, long time ago.

We never stopped running until we saw the same train station Kris and I took to get here. Only then did we stop sprinting. The same old man was leaning against the train, staring at the sky. When he saw us, he nodded, expecting us to go by.

"Uh, sir, we want a ride, please." The train driver told us the prices and Carson began flipping through the cash. We weren't going far at all, so only $21.00 was taken out of our stash.

We boarded the train with $546.00. The train driver didn't take much notice of us. Carson sat in the front by himself and watched as the driver drove the train. Nathan and Selene sat together, and as Kris joined me, I whispered: "Isn't it weird the train driver doesn't remember us?"

Kris shrugged. "Why would he? Do you know what could happen in *five months*? Take our situation, for example."

"Yeah, but it's only five months. "Kris shook her head and settled into the chair. I watched the scenery go by and was about to take out my notebook when suddenly, smoke trailed by the window, and we went slower until we halted then came to a complete stop.

"Shoot!" the driver sprung up from his seat and opened the doors. Kristina and I exchanged glances. A tired-looking man came in.

"Well, folks," he announced, "Mr. Mackie needs to fix a broken engine, so I believe some people have to hop off while he does his business." He wiped his hands on his dirty blue overalls and sighed. "Should've taken care of that last week," he grumbled to himself.

Carson shot up. "No, we can wait," he insisted. We all gave him a look that said, *No, we can't wait.* We ended up getting off and stood in the grass. The sun was already almost out.

"How long do you think it'll take to fix it?" Selene asked.

"Hours, maybe," Mr. Mackie grunted, reaching down into the engine. "This needs time."

Nathan slapped the sides of his pants. "Great," he said. "It's over. Now we have to go back, get in trouble, and then get kicked out. Dead end." He kicked the ground.

"No way are we giving up now," I remarked. "We can walk, you know. There's nothing wrong with our legs."

Selene pointed to the north and commented: "I can see a store. We can't be that far away from town."

"Speaking of stores," Carson noted, "we might be stopping by one next."

"Why?" all four of us chorused.

"Um." Carson looked at us like we were doing something awkward. "There's no way anybody is gonna let us get very far looking like…this. You guys look like you just came out of the Great Depression, and I don't need to be in juvie court. So, we'll be stopping at the next clothing store to buy something decent, that a normal, modernized, teenager would wear. No…offence?"

"None taken," Nathan muttered.

Everybody was looking offended, so I stood up for Carson and exclaimed: "Wait, wait, wait, guys. I look forward to buying some new clothes. And there's no way the police will believe us if we look like this."

Everybody stared at me.

"Let's walk."

We trudged for about two miles until we reached a store that didn't look like it sold thousand-dollar outfits. The store was pink and white. We opened the door. *It's warm in here,* I thought, keeping on my jacket.

A woman was behind the counter. She was watching us but didn't say much. There was girls' clothing on racks. I quickly flipped through them. Eventually, the woman put down her phone, uncrossed her legs and walked up to us.

"Hello, can I help you?" she asked. "We'd like to buy some clothes," Carson answered when the rest of us stayed silent. He pulled out the stack of dollars to assure her.

The woman nodded. "Sizes?" she inquired. There was silence. Over the last few months, the only times I would be worried about my clothes was when I feared that the fragile thing would rip in two. I didn't have the faintest idea what my clothing size was. The woman (whose nametag revealed her name was Rachel) sighed. "This is gonna be a long morning."

"Are you ready yet? Come out!" Carson called. "It's been, like, twenty minutes. We have to get going!" I could hear squeaking curtains. I peeked through a tiny hole and saw Nathan and Selene come out at the very same time. Nathan was wearing a denim vest on top of a navy blue and white striped shirt with black jeans and red tennis shoes. Selene was wearing a yellow shirt with a smiling emoji on it, a white flowing skirt, strapped sandals, and a golden headband.

I insisted on being last, so Kris paraded out, decked in a black shirt with shining bumblebee yellow overalls with a black shirt. She had kitty ears on the top of her head, and the one, the only, almost identical-looking boots on her feet. Like the icing on a cake.

While everybody ooh-ed, I groaned: "C'mon, do you *seriously* have to wear *black*?"

"The overalls are yellow!" Kris protested. I rolled my eyes and strolled out, since it was my turn. Here I was, (probably the most transformed out of all of them) in a black and white striped shirt with a small jean jacket. I had sky-blue jeans and thick-soled light-pink boots, and a gold necklace with a heart charm. I also had white, gold-rimmed vintage glasses pushed into my hair. A white mini backpack was on my back. Last, but certainly not least, at the last moment I whipped a reindeer headband on my head. They were more realistic than I pictured. They even dangled with lights that turned on with the flick of a tiny, almost invisible switch.

The risk of my head being set afire, I didn't know, but until I smelled smoke, I wasn't taking this beauty off. Carson walked over to the woman. "What's the damage?"

"Fifty-nine, ninety-nine," the woman chirped. Carson handed her sixty dollars. "Do you want change?" Rachel asked.

"Yes, please." The woman rolled her eyes, walked over to her cash register, and handed a penny to Carson. "Ya'll look better than when you came in," the woman called as we were leaving, "better than the rags you were wearing before." Now, I rolled my eyes and whispered to Kristina: "Don't listen to her."

Our next destination was a place that served breakfast, lunch, and dinner. It was 9:00 in the morning and we were ready for some breakfast. We got a table outside in the blazing sun under a little umbrella. I ordered pancakes and eggs, Nathan waffles, Selene Greek yogurt and oatmeal, Kristina waffles as well and Carson glazed blueberry muffins with chopped hazel nuts on top. He still believed he was spoiled and pampered as he was inside The Diamond Square.

When we were done, no plate had anything left on it. The food had been heavy and, for the first time in a long while, it filled us up completely. Carson left $40.00 for the food and $10.00 as a tip.

"We still have an hour and forty-five minutes before we get on the train," Carson told us as we got up from the table and began walking away. "We can still explore."

We turned to each other and grinned.

The whole Downtown area was awesome. We saw a human mannequin who waved at us in front of a shop, saw a couple with the man walking five identical dogs and the woman pushing triplets in a stroller. The Diamond Square Gang with Carson went over to the ocean and had the most fun we could have without getting our clothes dirty or wet. Kris tried to stuff seashells in her pockets. We stopped by a bakery and got two of our favorite desserts. Nathan wanted to get a cake but that was a huge no-no. All the way, we tipped beggars and tried samples. All the while, Carson took photos, and more photos and even more photos. Sometimes I wondered how much trouble he would be in when he went back to his dad. Thirty minutes before we had to go to the train station, we were in front of the police station.

Feebly, Carson knocked on the door. When there was no response, he opened the door and motioned for us to follow him. The last thing I wanted to do was go into a police station without permission, but this was for freedom. I recognized the man sitting at the desk, looking husky and easily angered. I suddenly realized he was the same man who advised Carson and me to 'move it' when we went to make our report about the caged rat guys. Praying he wouldn't recognize us; I told Carson to go up to him. I saw the bucket of tickets and my eyes gleamed.

"Hello," Carson began once we were within talking distance. The man didn't say anything, just stared. Finally, he snapped: "Well, are you gonna talk or not?"

"Right, right," Carson stammered, "um, we want…uh, we heard…Here." He slapped twenty bucks on his desk.

"What's it for?" the guy grunted and stared at the money as if it were a bomb about to blow up any minute. "We want the tickets," Carson blurted, "and we're paying for it, too." He gestured towards the 20-dollar bill.

The man shook his head, pushed away the money and sat back.

"They aren't for sale."

"But…"

"Not for sale!"

"We really need them, though!" Selene interjected, her eyes already filling with tears.

"How many times do I have to say it? They aren't for sale. Chief's orders. Beat it!"

"Then can we talk to the chief?" Carson pleaded in pure desperation. The man sighed, picked up a red telephone, beeped some numbers, and then muttered: "Some minors want to see ya. 'Bout the tickets."

By the time we reached the train station, only $406.00 remained in our possession. The train station was underneath a glass roof with no doors whatsoever. Because they were so well known, the chief was familiar with our parents and didn't have a problem with handing over the tickets. We sat down on a deserted bench, and I pulled my diary as well as my pen out of my brand-new mini backpack.

We're at the train station, with snacks still left to eat, new clothes and…this sneak-out was better than I thought, because I might, just might have thought it would've ended horribly. Was I wrong?

The train is here.

CHAPTER 22

Reunion

Our tickets were punched, and we were allowed on the train. We were greeted with this question: "Do you have your parents or a guardian with you?" Of course, we said no.

"What are your ages?" the woman who greeted us asked.

"Fourteen," Carson started.

"Thirteen."

"Thirteen."

"Twelve," Nathan ended.

The woman nodded. "Then I'll be your guardian for this train trip, thank you." The seats were in rows of three. Ari, Carson, and I sat in three chairs and Nathan and Selene sat together with a stranger on the right side of Nathan. The train was long. The last passenger was short because I couldn't see the top of his head.

"I'll have to ask you to move somewhere else," our train guardian said to the stranger next to Nate. "There's a minor on board and I want her to sit there." The stranger was understanding and sat somewhere else.

When the person arrived, I was surprised to see that she was familiar. Kristina was eyeing her as well. Once the train pulled off, everybody was already absorbed in something. Not long after we pulled out of the train station our train guardian was pulled aside, and the little girl got out of her seat, came over to us and whispered: "Come."

"Why?"

"I need to use the bathroom." She tugged on my hand. I stared at Ari and she shrugged. Reluctantly, I got up with Ari right behind me as the girl towed me over to the restroom. She didn't even go in, just stood there, eyeing Nathan and Selene, who were looking at us. She began motioning for them to come as well.

I was annoyed. "Why do you need four people to watch you use the bathroom?" I demanded as Nathan and Selene began coming our way.

"I don't need to use the bathroom." My face flooded with confusion, and Ari looked at me. I took a step back, even though I shouldn't be afraid of a little kid.

Once Nate and Selene arrived, she whispered: "I need to tell you something." Her voice was charming, terrifying, and suspicious at the same time.

We didn't even answer before she could say the most haunting words that have ever entered my ears: "I set fire to your apartment." There was a silence.

"What?" Ari asked after a while.

"I set your home on fire," the girl repeated, "I did it. I was responsible for it all." She smiled, and I began to think the kid had a hole in her head.

"Do I know you?" I interrogated. "I'm the Girl Scout who gave you the cookies," the girl recited cheerfully. "And after I put them on the counter, I set fire to your apartment and that's why it's gone now."

"What is she talking about?" Nathan questioned. "Is this some sort of joke?"

"Did you have a permission slip, when you forced the cookies on us?" Ari inquired. I didn't know what to say.

"No. I only gave the cookies to you." I had been a Girl Scout long enough to know without a permission slip, you weren't allowed to sell any cookies. The girl was obviously with us when the fire happened, and she had given us cookies when we didn't want them, but…

"Perhaps I need to explain," she said. "It all began a long, long time ago. Daddy married this woman named Lia and for two years, they were happy until Mommy gave birth, which is when her health started going down the drain. Daddy pleaded to get paid early, but his boss refused. Daddy got aggressive and lunged at him. The case was brought to court, and there was only one witness, and of course it was stupid Mrs. Collins, and once she brought up her story, Daddy was laid off from his job. Fired!

"Now, they couldn't pay medical bills as well as house bills. Daddy didn't want Mommy to know, but eventually she did, which put a lot of strain on her and their relationship. Sick as she was, she wanted a divorce and went to live with her family instead. Daddy blamed his boss, the lawyer and Mrs. Collins, but who would be the easiest target to get revenge on? Mrs. Collins of course.

The girl went on to say that Mr. Waite remarried Mrs. Sesmore, who he had known since high school. Not many knew of the marriage since Mr. Waite wasn't the most popular guy in town. And he had so little funds they had to arrange to have the wedding in a friend's backyard. Mrs. Sesmore, however, was determined to keep her family's last name, which was perfect, because she would be a major help in this project.

The little girl continued narrating: "Daddy and Mrs. Sesmore brought the Collinses to court, over and over, bringing up cases, pleading for justice. Nothing worked. The judge even threatened jail time if Daddy did not stop. Yet, he persevered. He wrote letters to the Collinses asking them to admit the truth. The Collinses who, sadly, were incredibly famous, brought it to the media. Threats, scariness, all sorts of foolishness. Daddy had a choice to either leave them alone or face the consequences. One day, Daddy was driving this car he borrowed from a friend when he happened to be right behind the Collinses' car. Angry and upset he tried to swerve around it but ended up swinging into the car! Outraged, another court meeting was called into session, and Daddy was charged with the damage of the Collinses' car, twelve thousand, as well as the friend's, six thousand dollars.

"Daddy couldn't get a job," so Mrs. Sesmore found a job, and a few months later they could pay off the Collinses' car, but not for their friend. Daddy decided enough was enough and went out of town. A man has his limits, you know. He started an orphanage to make a little money far away from the place where most people knew him."

The couple had tried to persuade Carson to start the fire at Aunt Maybelle's apartment, but he wasn't the type. He was twelve at the time, so he knew better. So, they decided to adopt a younger child, Gracie, because they were able to influence her to do whatever they wanted.

Then news that Mr. and Mrs. and Mr. Collins had passed away became the talk of the town.

At first, all was good, until they started to wonder about us, Ari, and me and where we were. When news spread, that we lived with our aunt now, that's when they sent Gracie to "take care of things," with the fire. Mr. Waite sent his younger brother to put us on the streets when no guardians were around. Once we were on the street, Mr. Waite thought we were gone, until we showed up at The Diamond Square.

The worst part is that mostly everybody (except the police chief here) thinks we're either dead, burnt to cinders in the fire or kidnapped… one of the three. Nobody knows we're alive and thriving. Everybody believes we're buried under some tombstone. I can imagine how Natalie, who left just before the fire, must be thinking we were scorched to pieces or Aunt Maybelle, who probably thinks we've been kidnapped must feel. All guilt must be on their shoulders. And it isn't even their fault; not at all.

Mr. Waite also committed lots of crimes, some he might've done, others he was accused of that he might not have done. Yep, the man I hated so much and thought I would never get revenge on has turned out to be the closest thing to a fugitive as you can get.

Ari left us and went to get Carson. When they returned, Ari pointed to the girl and asked: "Does this girl ring a bell? Happen to know her, by any chance?"

"We don't have time for reunions," the girl interrupted, "it's time for business."

"We?" I stepped in front of Carson. "So, you're with her now? What's gonna happen next?"

"He's not with me," Gracie put in quickly, "who I mean are Daddy and Sesmore. They're waiting for you at the next train station." There was a silence.

"They knew we snuck out?" Ari asked softly. Another silence was confirmative. I began waving my hand in Carson's face. "How else would they know we snuck out!" I exclaimed, trying hard to keep my voice steady, since passengers were already giving us strange looks. "This scene is literally screaming it!"

"Tracking devices, security cameras, microphones," Gracie recited, "Do you really think you're the first ones to try this?"

"Yup!" Nathan cried, breaking another pause. "We're definitely going to die now! How could I ever think this could go right?" He was now pacing back and forth.

"You mean, Mr. Waite and Mrs. Sesmore are waiting at the next stop?" I cried.

Gracie nodded. Our train guardian came back and told us that we really needed to get to our seats, now. "But…" I tried to protest. The train guardian wouldn't have it. She directed us to our seats and instructed us to buckle up.

"All right, folks, we're about ten more miles until our next stop," the train driver announced as the scenery roared by the window. I fidgeted for the billionth time. Ari was thinking, and she leaned over and whispered: "We need to get her to leave." Meaning our train guardian.

"Yeah, but how?"

Ari paused for a moment, then leaned over and commented to the lady: "Excuse me, but I left my phone in the bathroom. "Can you get it for me, please?" The woman sighed and began walking. Just seconds after, Ari sprang up and motioned for me to follow her.

Before anybody could stop her, she opened the train driver's cabin, and I went inside and shut the door. The train driver glanced at us quickly, before turning back to the road. He was a man, probably in his thirties, with brown hair and sweat dripping down his forehead.

"What are you doing here?" he snapped, still facing forward. "You can't be in here, it's not safe. Get back to your seats immediately." I anxiously grasped his chair and pleaded: "You have to stop the train!"

He shook his head. "I don't want to be the cause of a mob of angry passengers. Besides, we're in the middle of nowhere! Seats, now."

"There are buildings and people, we can navigate," Ari cried, not backing down. "You don't know who is waiting for us at the next train station, and you don't want to be the cause of what's gonna happen. Trust me, you don't."

The train driver wouldn't be moved. I grasped his shoulders, which made him swerve a bit. He slapped my hands off harshly with one hand and spat at how dangerous that was.

I didn't care. "I'll do anything to make you stop this train, and now!" I meant it too.

The guy looked like he was going to say no, but then had a more thoughtful look on his face. Finally, he said: "Well…I'll let you out *if*…You can make those people laugh."

"Laugh?" Ari and I chanted.

"Yeah, laugh." The train driver smiled at the road. "Go ahead, don't be shy. If you wanna leave so badly." Ari and I began slowly evacuating the cabin. Make the people laugh? What a strange request! People always told us we were hilarious, but I wasn't sure we were comedians. As we made our exit, the train driver cackled into his walkie talkie: "Hey Sam, come and take over the train while I go on break. I wanna see this."

Once we got out, we were face-to-face with our guardian, who didn't look happy. "There weren't any phones in the bathroom," she stated accusingly. She told us to sit down, until we informed her that if we got the people on this train to laugh, we could get off before the next stop.

She grunted but sat down in my chair to watch. Everybody began eyeing us. I got nervous, and twiddled my fingers around, staring at the floor. The train driver was eyeing me, shrugging and his whole expression was telling me: *Well, are you gonna do this or not?*

I pointed my finger at him and shook my head. People turned their heads, saw nothing, and then looked back at me, their faces showing they thought I was crazy.

"Hi, I and my sister are going to do a comedy act," Ari announced for the two of us. "I hope you enjoy. And if you hear a joke, please laugh, even if it isn't funny." There was murmuring that sounded like conversation.

We started telling all kinds of jokes. The knock-knock ones, the ones that work only with kids and not so much with adults, and even ones we found in books. In desperation, we sang a duet, which a quarter of the people sang along to (and which a boy began snickering heavily at).

"Two and a half miles left to the train station," a crackly voice exclaimed, "two and a half miles left to the train station. Two youngsters had better clear the stage. Clear the stage."

"I'M KRISTINA COLLINS!" I screamed, folding my hands over my heart. "And this is my twin sister. And we really need your help. Our mom and Dad were Truman and— "A phone went flying into my face. Stars glowered around me. Once recovered, I held my cheek and stared at the phone on the floor—liquid with pink glitter—with my mouth ajar.

The train driver was laughing so hard he looked like he might just suffocate. I picked up the phone, shook it at the crowd and cried: "OKAY! But that has gone too far!"

A young woman was giving me the eye, and I marched up to her. She looked at me and whispered: "Oops. I'm sorry, but I looked up very much to Mrs. and Mr. Collins and was a fan of the twins. I don't appreciate impostors."

Outraged, I aimed the phone to slam against the wall close to her, but it bounced right into the lady's face, barely missing her eyes. Whoops! I covered my mouth. I guess that's why the counselors took me out of archery camp.

There was a gasp of shock. Before the woman could express her rage, or I could apologize or before a big fight could break out, the train driver caught me and Ari by the collar, the doors opened, and he shoved us out and practically giggling to death said: "Don't you ever come back on this train." Nathan, Selene, Gracie, and Carson were out right before the doors closed and the train drove out to the west. "Half a mile to the next stop," I heard before the voice was drowned out by the train wheels.

"That…was…awesome…I…" But before Nathan could say anything else Gracie shouted: "OVER HERE!"

We all turned to our left and saw Mrs. Sesmore and Mr. Waite running towards us. "RUN!" one of us screamed, and we all began sprinting to the east. With Mrs. Sesmore and Mr. Waite hot on our heels, I ran as fast as I could without passing out.

Carson was in the lead with Ari next, then me, Nathan and then Gracie. Selene brought up the rear. She began shrieking because one jump and Mr. Waite could take her down. I looked back for a second and saw Mr. Waite bring down a distressed Selene. She began screaming for her life, which attracted much attention.

Attagirl, Selene. Make yourself seen.

"Um, excuse me sir," a woman began strutting towards us. "But, what in heaven's name are you doing to these children?"

Mr. Waite let Selene go free and then stammered: "These…these are my children." He walked over, slammed his palm on Carson's head and whispered: "Right?"

Carson didn't say anything. The woman nodded. "Right, right," she said, "Do you have any proof?" Mr. Waite stood tall and announced: "I own an orphanage. These kids snuck out, I have the right to bring them in and put them back in order."

The woman studied Mr. Waite long and hard. "I think I know you," she grunted, "who are you again…OH WAIT! You're the…you're the…" She began snapping her fingers rapidly. "I know you! You're the *Waite Guy*. The Collinses number one hater. Oh my gosh, the world *HATED* you back then!" Waite turned pink and snapped: "Alright, that's quite enough, I…"

"Oh, man," another man cried from the street. "You got in so much trouble the news channel might as well have gotten you a show!"

"And you ran away from your problems and here you are now," the same strutting woman muttered, looking him up and down. "Chasing innocent children down the block." Mrs. Sesmore had already made her exit and Mr. Waite commented: "Well, it's been nice reconnecting to the world after all these years, but I must go now. Come along, Carson."

"No, I don't think so." The woman stopped him in his tracks and pulled out a modern flip phone. "I don't think I'll let a fugitive get away." She began beeping and dialing, and then put the phone to her ear. "You know, I'm just gonna call 9-1-1 really quick." She turned to Carson. "And maybe Child Protection Services as well."

That did it. Mrs. Sesmore and Mr. Waite began running hard down the street. Now, they were officially fugitives. The woman told Carson to stay with her until the Child Protection Services arrived, and the rest of us could go on with our day.

This was awkward. I didn't know whether to say goodbye or just run. Either way I felt like I didn't have enough time. The woman was pacing, talking to the police casually, as if nothing was happening.

"Uh, sorry about your dad," Ari remarked. "And your sister," I added.

"It's okay. I knew my sister was evil."

I knew it was my turn. Eyes and nose burning, I managed to utter, "See you around…?" Ari looked down. Carson waved weakly, seeing our pain. We turned around, stared at each other, and kept running down the street.

I can't keep on doing more-than-likely forever goodbyes like this. I'm never gonna see him again, the guy who gave us our one and only chance to be free, almost a second chance to really live life; and I had only said three words to him?

How am I going to say goodbye to Nathan and Selene?

CHAPTER 23

Goodbye, Hello

Selene and Nathan lived together before they wound up at The Diamond Square. Nathan lived with Selene's family. They had gotten lost one day and when The Diamond Square was the only option they had, they took it.

Selene's mom answered instantly. When she came, we all piled into the car. She was talking to Selene all during the car ride, asking endless questions about what happened to them while they were gone, were they ever mistreated, did they had enough to eat, etcetera, etcetera.

While Selene was talking, I asked Nathan: "Are your parents dead? Are you an orphan too?"

He looked at me like I was crazy. "No…"

"Are they lost?"

"No."

I thought for a moment.

"Well, then, what happened to them?"

"I don't know."

"When our parents were alive, we used to go everywhere. We used to have these nights when we watched a movie or played dominoes or something like that," I murmured dreamily.

"Oh, wow, sounds like you were spoiled," Nathan remarked sarcastically. I crossed my arms.

"Ha, ha, very funny, but we had huge blasts. Did you have times like those before?"

"When?" Nathan asked.

"With your parents," I said.

"No…"

"Why not?"

"I dunno."

"Here's the thing," I suggested, "I think you do know. And I also think that you're holding out on me."

There was silence, then… "When I was living with Selene,-every time her siblings were trying to go to sleep, we would put Mentos into a Coke bottle and splatter them." He grinned at the memory. "We did that a lot at school too, splattering teachers and students until a teacher threatened us with detention."

Selene finally took a break from talking with her mom and was now talking to Kristina. "How long were you at The Diamond Square?" I asked after a while.

"A year or two before you got there…"

"And you're twelve now, right?"

"Yup."

"So, you came there when you were ten. Hey, I just realized something cool that Kris and I and you have in common."

Nathan looked at me. "What?"

"That we both lived with our aunts until our lives turned upside down," I observed, proud of myself for noticing. Nathan nodded like it was nothing.

"You know, before I used to be scared of you," he said quietly. I stared out of the window.

"Why?" I asked. I had always tried to be as open as possible, to make people feel at ease when they met me. I never would've guessed Nathan feared me if he hadn't just told me.

"I don't know. Kristina too. Sorta…I could get use to Kris's hazel eyes pretty quickly. But…green eyes freak me out!"

"Why does my eye color freak you out?"

"Just…reminds me of someone." Nathan began playing with his shirt.

"Who?" Before he could answer, Selene's mom pulled into the parking lot where Aunt Maybelle had agreed to get us. As if reading my thoughts, Kristina murmured, "That's probably the happiest car in the world right now." I smiled and looked at her. *"For now."* I agreed.

Kristina snatched my phone and began dialing.

About ten minutes later, a black Toyota pulled up and we climbed into Aunt Maybelle's car. Aunt Maybelle isn't the kissy or hug-like type, but she still expressed her relief at seeing us.

Kasie was there too, but she acted as if she didn't care we had returned. She would be turning eight in just a couple weeks, she announced, since she thought we had forgotten.

Aunt Maybelle told us that our apartment had been restored to its original state. It was about an hour's drive away and so Kris and I filled the two of them in on every single detail of our adventure.

We told them about the parade, games we used to play, the unbearable times, the skimpy meals, Christmas and of course, the fire - because who could forget that? Kristina told them about every time she got hypothermia and gave a vivid recollection of her rage for the man who abducted us. She also told the latest story of the phone-throwing woman.

When Kris described the lady, Aunt Maybelle told us that she might be an old friend from grade school.

After a whole hour of non-stop talking, we arrived at our apartment. After taking the elevator we went up to our door and Aunt Maybelle dramatically flung it open. I marveled at the kitchen and living room with a lovely fireplace. A door led to a bathroom and another to a bedroom, which had a door that led to another bedroom.

One thing was missing. Pictures, stuff that only we saw, quotes, memories. I got an idea, dashed through both doors, grabbed something off the couch, returned to our (more than likely) bedroom and placed my journal on the bedside table. There.

The first step to really being home.

The news spread. Ariel and Kristina Collins were now officially back home, and not dead. Mr. Waite and Mrs. Sesmore were going to spend a few months in jail, while the orphans from The Diamond Square were sent to other less harsh orphanages. I don't exactly know what happened to Carson and Gracie, but they're definitely gone now.

Lately, reporters and local news channels have been asking us for interviews, on both TV and on the radio. Before the fire, we were known, but never like this.

It was only about nine days since the escape, and I decided to use Aunt Maybelle's computer and see if I could email Selene and Nathan. I crept out of my room and into her office. Kristina was trying to clean the stain she had accidentally got on one of her favorite shirts and Kasie and Aunt Maybelle were hanging out at the park. Ever since Kris and I have returned, she has felt the need to do less work.

I didn't find the address, so I exited out of 'mail' and noticed that Aunt Maybelle had Google open with the search bar revealing her search history.

The most recent search read: 'Are Helene and Turman Collins out of hiding?' Wait, what? I immediately clicked on the search tab and found a number of headlines. I clicked on the first one I saw.

Helene and Turman Collins Out of Hiding for Over 6 years???

After 6 whole years of being thought lost and or dead, living under false names while still trying to stay in touch with family, Mr. and Mrs. Collins have decided to return to their home. They have been invited to get interviewed by the famous TV show' It's Di' hosted by world-famous Diane Davis this summer...

Living in Albany, New York, the couple....

I heard a knock on the door and instantly closed the tab and turned the computer off. Kristina, who had wandered into the office, shuffled to the door and unlocked it, still wearing yellow gloves.

I got off the rolling chair, plopped my body on the couch and turned on the TV, flipping through channels as if I had been there for a while.

"Well, that was eventful," Aunt Maybelle huffed as she let go of Kasie's hand. "Hello Kristina."

"Hi." Kasie dug into her pockets and pulled out some mashed-up flowers. "I'm going to put them in my church dress pockets," she sang as she made her way to her room. Aunt Maybelle grinned and commented to Kris that she never told her to do that.

I got up and tried to make my escape to somewhere else when Aunt Maybelle addressed me. "Glad we're back, Ariel?" I whizzed past her, heading to the kitchen without answering her.

In the kitchen, a crumpled piece of paper was on the floor near the garbage bin. I opened it and stared at its contents. The lettering was in Aunt Maybelle's handwriting.

Cleveland to New York on bus- 4 hours 30 minutes

Cleveland to New York on plane-About 1 hour, 30 minutes???

Ticket for one: $364x2=$28

Shaking hands, I dropped the paper back on the floor. Not only had the past six years of my life been a lie, but now two people are coming here or going there, and Kris and I didn't even know? How could she do that?

I know Aunt Maybelle had said when we first came to live with her, she might not be able to tell us everything for our own safety, but this?

Who was coming? Who was going? Dad and Mom? Or Aunt Maybelle and somebody else? What if somebody else bad came and we were kidnapped again?

Who knew all she had been hiding if this was only one of the things on the list! I heard Aunt Maybelle taking off her coat and getting relaxed on the couch. I peeked a bit at her, and then pulled back, still clutching the paper. How could I ever trust her again?

What other secrets are you trying to keep?

CHAPTER 24

Epilogue

"And that's a rap!" somebody shouted. The cameras turned off and Ari and I prepared to go. Our interviewer was a woman with curly mahogany hair, who was wearing a watch that looked expensive but probably cut off her circulation. Her name was Lauren. Before the interview, I told her she should dye her hair purple, because she looks like the type of lady that'll look good with indigo locks. She laughed.

Lauren followed us out of the room. She had two business cards and gave one to each of us. On it was her name, the name of her studio, three telephone numbers you could contact her by and the address of the studio. A tiny picture of her topped it off.

Here we go again.

"It's such a blessing to have you guys here," Lauren repeated for the seventh time since we walked in. "I'm so fortunate. You know, if you ever, *ever* feel the need to come back, just dial up one of these phone numbers, *any* of the three, and I promise you two sugars I will get you on TV straight away."

Lauren's channel, how do I say this, was straight-up dying. Hardly anybody watched it anymore, and the second anyone who could boost her ratings showed up, she would sell her skin to keep them.

"Thanks, Mrs. Halle." Ari stuffed the card in her pocket. "But I'm not sure we'll have the time."

"We really must be going now," I interrupted. I was trying to get in the act. "I'm sorry, Mrs. Halle."

Lauren was desperate. "Oh, no! You are always free to call me Lauren, like I'm your big sister." She squeezed us in a big bear hug. "You don't mind that, right?"

"Nope!" Ari and I chanted, although we both had a serious, serious problem with all of that.

We skipped out of the building and caught the bus before Lauren could suggest anything else. We had only taken the interview to be nice.

Once safely on the bus, I said: "I can never get how she still manages to rope us into these things."

"She's the type you can never say no to," Ari sighed, looking at the blob of gum attached to the seat in front of us.

Natalie was no more. She hadn't died or anything like that, but moved away, far, far away, and Aunt Maybelle didn't know how to contact her to ask her to come back. Lately, she's been looking for nannies so she can go back into work full swing again.

I heard about my parents a couple of days ago by Ari, but neither of us told Aunt Maybelle what we knew, although we plan to do so, soon. In the meantime, we think about homework, schoolwork, and projects.

Somehow, Aunt Maybelle found an online learning program for Ari and me to use until we get to eighth grade. She keeps worrying we'll have to repeat the seventh grade since we haven't been in a real school for so long. However, I believe the things Mrs. Sesmore taught us at The Diamond Square paid off. We took an IQ test to see where we were at, and we were at our grade level, although just barely, which means we might be in the B range for a while, but hey, at least we wouldn't fail!

The biggest news in town is about our parents which means we aren't referred to as "orphans" anymore. I mean, our parents aren't dead so what's the point in calling us something that we aren't anymore? But that title had a nice ring to it, and sometimes I still like to call myself an orphan, even though I am really not one anymore.

Glossary

Smothering: Completely covered 11

Behind: Informal use for a person's buttocks 12

Off her rockers: Euphemism for mental instability 12

Whooshing: Suggested sound made by the hair dryer 22

Slenderman: A fictional character created by Eric Knudsen.
By way of description, he is a thin, unusually tall humanoid with a
featureless head and face who wears a black suit. 25

About the Author

Arianna Miller, an avid reader and a budding musician, is an amazing twelve-year-old, who is currently an outstanding seventh grader at one of the Bahamas' premier high schools - Queen's College.

Arianna's keen interest in the written word was evident during her homeschooling years up to second grade and was further nurtured by her teachers as she progressed through primary school.

This multi-talented author's achievements are many and varied. As a fifth grader, she received Honorable Mention as a finalist in the Bahamas Laws of Life Annual Essay Competition, and as a sixth grader, she participated in spelling bees at both the school and district levels.

Other notable sixth-grade experiences include being named Student of the Year and representing her school in the line-up of students having an audience with the Duke and Duchess of Cambridge, now the Prince and Princess of Wales during their recent visit to The Bahamas in March of 2022.

Arianna has a range of hobbies; among them are reading, swimming and playing the piano.

However, it was in 2020 when the whole world was in lockdown, that the then ten-year-old began to realize her dream of writing her book which she completed approximately one year later.

Her success at writing does not prevent her from being an active member of her church, Evangelistic Temple (Assemblies of God), where weekly she interacts with peers and participates in the music ministry serving as keyboarder in the youth band.

Arianna's spirit of volunteerism comes to the fore when she participates in the annual Christmas holiday gift-giving to children in inner-city communities.

She is certainly a role model for her peers! It is Arianna's wish that through this novel other young writers would be inspired to "find their voice" and develop their talent.

Arianna lives with her proud parents, Diarra and Velma Miller and her brother, Nicolas.